STEPHEN LONGSTREET

Sons and Daughters

G. P. PUTNAM'S SONS
New York

G. P. Putnam's Sons
Publishers Since 1838
200 Madison Avenue
New York, NY 10016

Library of Congress Cataloging-in-Publication Data

Longstreet, Stephen, date.
Sons and daughters.

I. Title.
PS3523.0486S6   1987   813'.54   87-13090
ISBN 0-399-13242-2

Typeset by Fisher Composition, Inc.

Printed in the United States of America
1   2   3   4   5   6   7   8   9   10

To my friend, now gone
John Collier
In recall of younger days when we couldn't age

How sharper than a serpent's tooth it is
To have a thankless child!
SHAKESPEARE, *King Lear*

Book One

PRIDE

Chapter One

The Fiores were giving a ball, a celebration of the liberation of Paris from the Germans. The guests were shaking hands, slapping backs, merrily eating good food, drinking and dancing. Songs and laughter filled the big stone house on its cliff overlooking the Pacific. There were young people—off-duty officers in fresh-pressed Navy and Army uniforms flirting with young women—and older citizens remembering past wars as they toasted this present one, some recalling their visits to the City of Light with mention of Gertrude Stein and Isadora Duncan, of afternoon cocktail hours at the Paris Ritz; others spoke of their husbands or sons with Patton's tanks someplace loose on an end run to the Rhine.

Gregory Fiore, the host, stood near the grand staircase, a small glass of brandy in his hand, overlooking the dancers. He, at fifty, was thinking of how many now middle-aged, cosmetic-aided women he could have slept with and hadn't, *and* the few he had. As an aging widower of two years, Gregory thought more about years gone by than about the present or the future. But as the senior heir to the banks that made up the Pacific-Harvester's system, he realized that the present and the future were paramount now—there were not enough mature Fiores to take over a major part in management or sit on the board of directors.

A woman screamed on the dance floor, a scream that turned to laughter. Gregory smiled. Someone had slipped an ice cube down her back. Two girls, followed by two young naval officers, disappeared into the library and closed the fumed oak doors behind them. Jorgen Dalgaard, a round man, was the bank's lawyer, and Sirko Girazain, a stick of a fellow, of Coastshore Bank, were lighting cigars at the bar. Gregory Fiore waved over the din of the band.

When his grandfather, the founder of the Fiore fortune, had built this stone house, Gregory had liked parties, balls and galas. But now he was sad—too many memories.

He was just beginning to recall images of his own return from that 1917–1918 war when his daughter Maude, co-hostess of the event, came up the grand staircase smiling, her long blond hair pulled up in a bun with a curl over one eye.

"May I request this dance?"

"Not tonight, Maude. There are so many eligible dance partners down there."

"Only Navy studs, all hands. Come on, Dad, just one spin?"

He shook his head, and with a kiss and a wave she was off. He watched her move in that swinging wonderful way, and recalled her mother, his wife Belle, now dead for two years. Some weathered hulk of a Navy commander seemed to envelope his daughter as the music went into an Irving Berlin tune. In the gardens great iron baskets of glowing charcoal warmed the night. The guests cheered as, beyond the bay, bursts of fireworks blossomed in the blue-purple sky, and clusters of colored fires expanded and sank away to be renewed from other directions. All of San Francisco was celebrating the liberation of Paris. *"Le bonheur semble fait,"* yelled a fat dancer, her mascara running down her cheek, *"pour être partagé."*

Cody Hutton was at Gregory's elbow with a fresh glass of brandy. Cody Hutton was called by some a butler, by some a valet and by others a hoodlum bodyguard. He was a hammered-down "mick," as he called himself, the nephew of Old George's long-gone Eddie Hayes.

"Georgie come yet?" Gregory asked Cody.

"Not yet. He's driving up from L.A. with some pals."

Gregory frowned. "Kids and cars." He took a sip of the brandy, savored it and swallowed. "Cody, he's not to use any of the cars in the garage."

Georgie, named after his great-grandfather, Old George, was a student at Irvine, aged fifteen and reckless with cars. He was picked up at Carmel driving his uncle Buckley's Mercedes without permission.

Gregory handed his brandy glass to Cody. "Cut off the music at one, Cody, and if anyone is upstairs, well . . ."

"Yes, sir. I'll see that everyone is properly dressed and on their way, sir."

Gregory Fiore smiled and tapped Cody on the shoulder. The mick was a bit wobbly—must have broken the rule of no sly drinking during social events at Cliff House. Well, thought Gregory, it's liberation night.

"Wake me up when Georgie gets in."

As he went up the grand staircase, Gregory thought its old rose carpeting, walls of teak and Art Nouveau carvings were a bit ornate, but Old George had built Cliff House the way he wanted.

At the top of the stairs Gregory paused, breathing slowly.

13

Dr. Steinman had said, "Greg, it's just a murmur, not a harmed heart; but don't go overdoing it."

Dalgaard, the bank's lawyer, had come up to Gregory with his paunch carefully hidden by well-designed evening clothes; his sky-blue eyes behind dark-rimmed glasses always seemed half-asleep, Gregory thought, like a wise old turtle dozing.

"A good party, Gregory. Real Rothschild bubbly!"

"From George's wine cellar. The remains for very special occasions."

Gregory never trusted lawyers, but he admired Jorgen Dalgaard.

The lawyer took a folded letter from an inner pocket of his evening jacket and handed it to Gregory.

Gregory took the letter; it was on yellow paper and folded too many times. "Do you think it's the real thing, Joe?"

"No. Not until she can prove herself." The letter was postmarked from Paris. "You never heard your uncle Fred say anything about him and this actress Inez Cortez having a child?"

"I don't think so. Joe, it was a long relationship. She never tamed down and she drove him nuts. But they were passionate for each other."

"Didn't he—I seem to remember—kill her?"

"No! Nothing like that. Some stranger murdered her—the usual Hollywood story. She was a star, not a mother."

The lawyer was looking up at the family portrait at the top of the stairs. "Jesus Christ, G.F., I feel like saluting the flag every time I see this picture."

It was a huge, well-lit painting in a heavy gold frame, done by John Singer Sargent sometime after the great San Francisco earthquake and fire. In the center, flowing cigar in hand, was Old George himself. In a dark banker's suit, white-piped waistcoat laced with a gold watch chain, the dark Italian looked serious, proud and wise. On each side of George were his two sons, Charles (Gregory's father) and Frederick (Uncle Fred).

"Nostalgia got you, Joe?" Gregory laughed.

The lawyer bit off the head of his cigar and lighted it. "Which is your old man?"

"Charles, on the left. He opened the Sky Dome oil fields in Texas with George's backing."

He looked back at the painting. In those days the real heir was to be Ramon Velasquez, the son of Old George's sister Irene. Ramon had that dark handsome Mediterranean look, almost Indian. The wisest of all, he was the first to die. In the painting he was standing just a bit to one side.

My old man, thought Gregory. Those years in the Panhandle before we brought in the first gusher. That's when the big oil boom started. Old George knew his sons couldn't carry on the banks. Freddie didn't even try—he'd rather be the womanizing playboy of the 1920s. His son, Buckley Fiore, who had had a wild start in life, was now moving with a Patton tank division somewhere outside of Paris. Gregory frowned. The letter indicated a half-sister for Buckley.

Greg turned to Jorgen Dalgaard. "Let's put Buckley in charge of our Paris branch."

"For now, let's just hope he keeps his head down in that tank of his. Good night, Greg."

". . . Night."

Gregory stared up at the painting once more and focused on Ramon. The best of us all. And yet he leapt from the deck of the *Mauretania* in that Liverpool-to-New York crossing. So cool, so wise, so civilized—he really missed Ramon.

Gregory went into his study and turned on his two favorite blue-green glass lamps, which made a calming atmosphere, like an aquarium. From below came the muffled sounds of departing guests, the bark of motorcars and fragmented farewells.

He sat very still at the ornate, flat-topped desk, and dozed off. He dreamed he was a large fish in the sea. He could hear the waves splashing against the cliff. He was breathing with gills in a wet, submerged world, and then a form walked toward him . . . "Uncle Ramon!" he cried out, but the words hadn't formed into sound in that deep, watery universe. Ramon was smiling that polite smile, his thick, ink-black hair floating now. Ramon held out his hand, and Gregory saw the flesh was gone. Between the finger bones, tiny white fish swam in and out. Gregory woke with a start and stared at the blue-green glass lamps, horrified at the dream. Cody Hutton came in with a robe over his arm.

"Fell asleep, did we now?" Cody bent down. "Oh, you dropped this. Can I dispose of it?"

Gregory took the folded letter from Cody.

"A successful party, sir. Just a window busted in the lower sunroom, and someone carried off a silver cigarette box. Everything else is hunky-dory." Cody said good night, left the study and closed the door behind him.

When Cody left, Gregory rose from the desk and stretched; when he was tired, his joints hurt. He went to a window and said very softly, "Hunky-dory . . . hunky-dory."

At the bottom of the garden on the path stood Georgie Fiore holding up a bottle of brandy. "I had it stashed under the gazebo."

"Wouldn't your old man miss it?" his friend, Chauncey, remarked.

"Don't be a jerk, Chaunce, he has slatters of the stuff. Come on, have a nip."

At fifteen, Georgie looked different from the other Fiore men, who were dark. He had blond hair like his mother, Belle.

Chauncey took a sip from the bottle and coughed. "Oh, sure, prime stuff, eh, Georgie?"

"You betcha." Georgie smirked.

They took turns sipping and showing off. From someplace in the garden they heard shaking and rustling among the bushes.

Georgie gave what he considered his best leer. "Somebody's getting theirs."

"Let's bushwack them!" whispered Chauncey. His eyes were glazing over.

"Oh, hell, why spoil their fun." Georgie took another sip and wiped his mouth with the back of his hand. "Truth now, you ever *done it?*"

Chauncey tried to sound like a man of the world affected by brandy. "Oh, sure. Plenty, believe me, Georgie boy. Plenty."

"No shit, really?"

"Would I lie to a future frat brother?" Chauncey was slurring his speech.

Georgie said, "Of course not. I tried it once with Agnes, the maid. But that doesn't count, I guess." He made the gesture of grasping his left biceps, fist up.

"Twenty-dollar quiff, I've had a few." Chauncey gloated.

"When did you start, Chaunce?"

"Oh," he said with a vague wave of a hand. "I was twelve. An aunt came to visit us."

"When I go to Yale, I'm going to hang out at the Old

Howard, the burlesque joint. French girls, the whole works."

The brandy had now gotten to them and they fumbled their words.

"Yale? That's a long way off, buddy."

"Yeah. Dad wants me to be premed. But I want to go out on digs . . . archaeology stuff . . . artifacts . . . relics . . . I'm going to toss my cookie . . ."

"Me too . . ." Chauncey's eyes widened.

They both ducked into the bushes and were sick, and afterward they stared at each other and laughed.

"Georgie, old boy . . . we better stick to beer."

They listened to the last car leaving the main drive. From nearby in the dark shrubbery came an ascending sound of lovemaking.

"I lied about my aunt; we just played around."

"Oh, Lord, that's potent brandy . . . I was showing off, too . . . Agnes the maid just gave me a slap in the face and threatened to tell my father if I ever tried *that* again."

After a while, feeling drained and dizzy, they sat in the grass, sucked in the cold air and held their stomachs. The lovers in the garden had finished, and as they were going, they laughed and shouted cheerful obscenities to each other. The two boys closed their eyes as the last few fireworks tore hot colors in the sky. The boys just winced painfully.

It was almost three A.M., and the celebration of the liberation of Paris was over.

18

Chapter Two

On weekends Maude and Georgie came home to Cliff House. Both were attending private schools. Before the war Fred's children, Buckley and his sister Penny, and her husband Harry—a very successful songwriter and musician—would come for family gatherings and holidays. The ornate coach house seemed to show disdain for the intruding automobiles: Buckely's jacked-up old car, Maude's Packard roadster, Cody Hutton's raspberry-colored Model A Ford, and Gregory's staid Lincoln.

Georgie and Chauncey climbed up the stairs to Georgie's bedroom, just down the hall from where his father was sleeping. They fell fast asleep without undressing.

The following morning the sun shone brightly. Awake and gathering himself back to reality, Gregory dressed. He wondered if Georgie had made it home safely and if Cody had tried to wake him up as he had promised. He slowly walked downstairs to the dining room, where a pot of coffee and his cup waited on a silver tray with a small crystal plate that held his morning vitamins and a bowl of freshly sliced fruit.

Cody set the morning *New York Times* and *The Wall Street Journal* before him. Gregory had them flown out to Cliff House every day.

"I take enough pills to rattle when I walk."

"My mother always said a little Jameson whiskey is the best medicine. Never bedridden a day in her life," Cody remarked.

"Did Georgie come home last night?"

"Heard him come in with his pal, Chauncey. I figured you were fast asleep—that party was a real shindig. They're probably still sleeping. I haven't heard a peep from the bedrooms."

"And Maude?"

"Got up at the crack of dawn to ride her horse at the ranch."

The *Times*'s war news was going well, but too damn slow. Gregory hoped it wouldn't go into the winter. He hated to think of Buck shaking out his guts in Patton's army tank. He turned to the business section; the American cost of living was up thirty percent. Pacific-Harvesters had gained a quarter, and steel was unsteady with the end of the war in sight.

Cody was pouring him another cup of coffee. "Looks like the National League St. Louies are favored to take the World Series."

"I noticed the *Times* sports section was missing," Gregory muttered.

"I knew J.P. Morgan's butler once. He told me he used to have to iron the New York newspapers every morning like shirts before handing them to the old fart."

There was a thump at the front door.

"That will be the mail." Cody shuffled out to the front hall.

Gregory spooned up his sliced fruit and thought how amusing and exciting his own war days were, forgetting how, in reality, it had been miserable.

Cody was at his side with a silver tray that held a dozen letters. Gregory waved off the servant and picked up one letter in a pale blue flimsy envelope. He recognized the stiff, scratchy handwriting with no slant to it, showing a strong character and not much education. He smiled at his interpretation; actually he didn't believe in judging character from handwriting.

The letter itself was written on cheap lined yellow paper, the kind found in school notebooks.

Mon cher Mr. Gregory Fiore:

You must not have gotten the letter I sent to you before Paris was taken by deGaulle. So I repeat now as the service of mail is better. My name is Anita la Fiore. I have been living in Paris during the occupation by Hitler and studying the art of singing at the Académie de l' Opéra. I am the daughter of your Uncle Frederick Fiore and the cinema star Inez Cortez. I have the birth documents. I was born on April 22, 1922, at the Hospital of Mary's Mercy in Tamaulipas, Mexico. I was raised by my aunt, Concepción Desuza. But all this I can fill in for you later. I have had a hard time of it during the war. I have little money and eventually will not be able to continue studying at the Opéra. So, I am asking for your help.

I write you the truth. There is no one else to turn to. You must have mercy in your heart for one who has so much talent. This is not the modest way to write of oneself, but my writing of English is clumsy. I do the best I can with it. Please send me as much money as you see fit—and have faith in me—I am Fred's daughter and therefore your cousin. But do not send for me. I cannot leave here. My address: En casa with some people called Balbac, 12 rue St. Didier, Paris.

Anita la Fiore

He looked down at the letter and thought of Uncle Fred, so jolly, so warm, so foolish. A kind man who handed out happiness like calling cards. He thought of Inez Cortez, the passionate actress of screen romances and longtime mistress of Uncle Fred. She was a woman with a hot temper and a carefree attitude toward life. Ignorant, uneducated, yet so wise in the ways of the world.

He told Cody not to bother getting his car ready. He'd walk to the bank this morning.

It would be a busy day, Gregory thought as he walked in the morning's sidewalk traffic toward the bank. He had to deal with the matter of reopening the branch bank in Paris and that damn letter from the girl who claimed to be his cousin. He was deep in thought when someone stumbled into his path. "Pardon me . . ."

He had been brushed by a drunken officer, a young lieutenant who looked more like a high school football player except for the large red scar across his left cheek and a bit of a sag in one shoulder.

"'Sh'all right, sport, 'sh'all right," he slurred.

He was very young and very drunk, and his head rolled about under the crumpled officer's cap.

"Can I get you a cab?" Gregory tried to get hold of the young officer's arm but was pushed away.

"I'm fine, jus' fine . . . going back to get shot in the ass in the Pacific . . . you know, off the fuckin' Japs . . . yes . . . you know . . ."

This time Gregory grabbed his arm and briskly walked

22

toward the bank. The boy went limp and saggy in the legs. The Fiore bank building was just half a block away.

"Got clear of the hospital AWOL . . . ha ha. All the stinking bodies . . . on Takua beach . . . they all . . . I mean . . . kids shot through the guts an' crying in the jungle and dying dying there . . . under fire next to me . . . and gone . . . you know . . . one minute rapidfire . . . fuck th' fuckin' war, and then you need a shovel to gather up what's left."

The boy groaned as Gregory rushed him up to the facade of the bank. At the entrance were posters for bond drives and a large two-story-high banner with stars for the bank employees who were at war.

He heard the boy retch and knew vomit would follow. He shouted at Andy Welton, the doorman.

"Welton, take over here!"

"Yessir, Mr. Fiore."

"Get him cleaned up, Welton, inside. Use Mr. Brownson's dressing room. And then show him into my office."

"Yessir, Mr. Fiore. Easy does it, lad."

Inside the vast two-story main banking area, Gregory admired the frosted etched glass and ornate bronze grillwork. The young girls and women who had replaced men off to the war were now part of the organization. He nodded greetings to a few of them and took the elevator up to his office. The young lieutenant reminded Gregory of himself, a drunken officer stationed in London in 1918 after the slaughter of two of his best friends in the attack at Saint-Mihiel.

His secretary, Stella Terry, came in with one rose, a writing pad and a pencil. Neat, well-dressed, the usual glance at her wristwatch, politely indicating he was late this morning.

"Good morning, Mr. Fiore."

"Good morning, Stella."

She placed the rose in a small vase and adjusted his appointment diary.

"Ten-o'clock meeting with Mr. Kelton, Mr. Brofnok, Mr. Florence."

"Mr. Flordale," he corrected her, "from our London office."

"Yes. Lunch at the Bankers Club, one P.M. Then your meeting with Mr. Dalgaard.

He smiled at Stella Terry, and realized she had started working for him as a delightful-looking redhead with fresh, peach-colored skin. She had been in awe of him then. Now, after twenty years, there was a crispness, a firm set to her mouth. What did he know of her private life? He knew almost nothing about her, and for years she had come in every morning with a flower, a pad and pencil, and an engagement list for the day.

"How are things with you, Stella?"

Her expression changed. "I manage with rationing." She smiled as she must have smiled a few thousand mornings as part of the procedure of her job.

"The morning mail is on your desk. Shall I have some coffee made?"

"No thanks, Stella. Get me the files on our prewar European branches."

He guessed Stella Terry must be close to forty. Still what Joe, his lawyer, would call "a dish."

He beat the desktop with a bronze letter opener, examined his mail. Most of it was routine letters and memos. Stella would see that it moved along to the various people in the proper departments.

He made comments on two letters with a red pencil, sat back and looked over his office. He looked up at the family photographs over the fireplace. His wife Belle in tennis attire at Santa Barbara. She had just won some club title. He stood proudly by her side behind Maude, who was holding little Georgie. There were photos of Buckley as a young man and his sister Penny; the whole family showed up to see Belle beat Santa Barbara's best at tennis.

Enough moping, Gregory thought as he took out the flimsy letter from Paris and put on his Churchillian half-glasses. He read it once more. Biting his lower lip nervously, he took up a sheet of bank letterhead. He wrote slowly: "Dear Buck:"

He must have been staring at the paper for some time; perhaps he had even dozed off. It often happened now. The intercom had woken him up.

"The gentlemen are here for the meeting, sir."

"Thanks, Stella. Have them come in."

A half hour later the office was a bit fogged by good Havana cigar smoke; Stella had served coffee and tea, and put out extra ashtrays. Gregory knew the men well. Milt Kelton was a Pacific-Harvesters stocks-and-bonds expert, a man with a thick head of graying hair, a small mouth, big shoulders and short legs. He had lighted his cigar with dainty care, guarding its growing ash. Martin Brofnok was a Canadian Zionist with worldwide knowledge of Argentine cattle, Chinese rice and Siberian sable, and Gregory had just read his impressive reports on South American tin and South African gold output. Brofnok had very firm ideas about where the bank should make large loans, small loans or no loans at all. His opinion on the reopening of the Paris branch would ultimately decide the matter as he waved his cigar about.

Barton Flordale was clearly British. He was thin, a bit horse-faced, his hair oiled and firmly parted in the middle. He wore a red waistcoat with a gold coin hanging at the end of a thin gold chain, which he constantly fingered as he talked.

"The French will always remain French. Democracy is a tradition with them, not a fact. We can reopen our old branch on rue St. Honoré with a couple of our best London chaps and Henri Satie, our agent there, and just wait to see how the show runs."

Gregory looked up at the three men seated around his flat-topped desk. "Barton, as soon as you say so, we'll open the Paris branch with no fanfare—just put your men in. Let Satie keep an eye on the French politicos. He'll know who's top dog."

"Oh, depend on that."

"You'll want someone American, though, to finally head it," said Kelton.

"You all know my cousin Buckley, Fred's boy?" He exhaled cigar smoke. To call Buckley a boy, hell, he's over forty. "Anyway he lived in Paris for some years. Before the war, he said he'd like to take it on."

"He's in Patton's army, isn't he?" asked the Englishman.

Stella Terry caught Gregory's eye and pointed to her wristwatch.

Gregory nodded. "Let's hope we can count on Buckley coming out of it soon."

"Oh, the bloody mess, it's almost over. In two weeks we get all our chaps across the Rhine and get that bugger Hitler done with . . ." said Brofnok.

Gregory said he hoped so because it looked like a cold winter, nodded to Stella and bid a good day to all three men. The Paris branch would reopen.

Gregory went to his bathroom, washed his hands and face, and looked at himself in the mirror. In movies, people looked into mirrors to find answers. He had often tried the mirror stare but got nothing back but deeper lines than the last time he looked.

Stella had opened the windows and cleared the office of most of the cigar smoke. But Gregory felt comforted by the aroma of good cigars mingled with that of the old wood-paneled walls and bookcases, and the faint odor of pepper-mint drops his grandfather kept in a desk drawer and handed to Gregory on his frequent visits as a small boy. But it was a ghost odor—a trick of memory; no peppermint-candy odor would survive the years since Old George had died.

Stella was on the intercom.

"Yes, Stella?"

"Lieutenant Scudder would like a moment."

"Scudder? Who the devil is—"

"He's the young officer you—"

"Yes, please send him in."

The young man came in slowly, looking somewhat pale, his tie loose. There were water stains on his uniform where some quick cleaning had taken place.

"Come in, come in. So your name is Scudder, Miss Terry tells me."

"Tad Scudder, sir." He closed his eyes, shook his head and opened them. "I made a goddamn jackass of myself."

Gregory motioned to a chair. "So you did. Well, you were pretty pissed there in the street. I didn't want the MPs to nab you."

"I had one too many drinks at the Union Club. All the jolly old boys were there—safe on their asses saying how wonder-ful we were to get shot up for them . . . oh, I'm sorry." He sat down. "I didn't mean to . . ."

"You're not sorry and I don't mind. We fat asses do have the best of it. Where are you from, Tad?"

"Red Bank, New Jersey. I didn't drink a hell of a lot at

Princeton before I got into the war. Oh, hell, my head."

Gregory sat back and smiled. "The old hangover." He flipped the intercom. "Stella, get something fizzy for the officer."

"Sir, I've had two of those already. I'm coming around. I made a mess and I'm sorry. I'm due to go down to Ord and train new officers in jungle warfare."

"How many people ask you how is it out there?"

"Everybody." The young officer tried to make an amused grimace but groaned instead. "Take hell and multiply it by a hundred, and you're close, almost. Jungle rot, land mines, booby traps, malaria."

"If you'll promise not to get lushed again, I'll take you to a fancy shindig at the Mark at five. Now go back to that dressing room and get some sleep. Oh, and have Miss Terry get your uniform dry-cleaned at some fast-service joint. She knows how to handle everything."

"You don't have to—I mean, thanks, but—"

Gregory said, "That's an order, Lieutenant. I'll come and pick you up at four-thirty."

Chapter Three

The December weather was very cold, and the air was thick, hiding the Germans, who were stepping slowly backward, and the Americans and the English, who were moving carefully forward.

The tank motors were often kept running through the night, as it was difficult to start them in the snowdrifts.

Major Buckley Fiore's tanks were in a grove of tall pines. There was no underbrush. Clearly it was a park that had once been part of an estate, as the burned out ruins of a chateau showed through a clearing. Close by were the remains of a bridge the Germans had blown up before planting some of their dead in a field with coal-scuttle helmets stuck up on bits of timber.

The general's trailer had been brought up among the tanks. The general and four of his staff sat over hot coffee, studying maps unfolded before them.

"It's snowing again," said Staff One.

"Damn—it's hell on tank treads," said the general, eyes

half-closed, his sharp-nosed face bent over the maps. Buckley unfolded another map showing more detail.

"They're old maps, sir, but the lay of the land hasn't changed much."

Staff One picked up a yellow report. "SHAEF says there are signs von Rundstedt is leaving scouts behind in his rear."

"What good would that do von Rundstedt? He'd be facing the wrong way," Buckley said.

The general broke his roll into bits and began to arrange the fragments and knives in a pattern. "I'm Hitler with my intuitive temperament: I want to surprise. Here's the Meuse, here's Antwerp, here's Brussels. I pack half a million men and supplies, cross the Meuse in force, separate the Allied armies and split them up. Force the British off course into Dunkirk. A very daring military move."

"Impossible. Too late." Buckley shook his head.

"Impossible! Buck, we're spread thin and the generals are goosing Monty to move."

There was an explosion nearby and far off a rattling series of explosions went off. The general closed the meeting and the men left, disappearing into a windy, driven snow. Buckley made his way to a small brick garden house, its shattered windows covered with ammo crate planks. Sergeant Jacob Ott was trying to keep a gas-pressure plat cooker from the wind as the door opened. He was boiling some sort of a mess in a G.I. issue pan.

"Yes, sir," said the sergeant, half-rising, pulling on the tan woolen scarf tied around his head and helmet.

"We will be moving soon, Jake. Keep my gear packed."

"Mail came, a bit delayed," said Ott.

Two newspapers at least a few months old, and two letters; one was from Gregory.

"Damn it, Jake, get some heat in that charcoal bucket."

There was little warmth in the few charcoal embers still aglow in an iron bucket stabbed full of holes.

"I'll go see if I can latch onto some ammo crates."

Buckley, keeping on his lined dogskin gloves, read his cousin's letter.

Dear Buck:

Let's hope the war soon goes faster than it's going. I had some winter fighting in 1917 near someplace you may be, and I know it's no Elks picnic. Maude and Georgie send you packages from time to time. They pray you get some of them.

I'm enclosing a photocopy of a letter from a woman who claims to be Uncle Fred's daughter by Inez Cortez. As you read you'll see she claims to have been in Paris all through the occupation. She just wants money from me—doesn't want to meet me, though. So if in the near future you get some leave and go to Paris, look and see what's what with this woman. We have a man, Henri Satie, in Paris, but I'd rather keep it in the family. A hell of a note if any of her claim is true. As Old George used to say to us boys, "We raise hell maybe, but no bastards."

As you know, your father left little personal estate. He was a wild spender, but what he couldn't touch were the trust funds left to you and your sister Penny. No so-called bastard can have any legal claims on those.

The town is bursting with activity—soldiers, sailors and all. The big talk is taking on the Japs; we no longer call them Japanese. The war in Europe seems to be boiling down.

Here we are planning to go camping. Maude, Georgie and me up to a lodge. Look forward to the day you get out of the service. I need you, Pacific-Harvesters needs you. The Fiores should be breeding more vice presidents.

How is it the world seems to be getting in these bloody messes every twenty years? Your sister Penny is doing fine—happy with Harry. He's doing well with his songwriting.

I have kept the sailboat in good condition in the bay and

31

the big sloop at Cliff House. Hope to see you soon. Cody sends his best.

> The best of the best to you,
> Greg

The wind was settling down. Buckley read the copy of the letter from the girl in Paris. Sounded phony. He put both of the letters away in his carryall and worried himself back to the war. He hoped the crankcase oil in the tanks wouldn't freeze.

Sergeant Ott was back with some broken-up ammo cases. Buckley shivered and lay down. He closed his eyes and listened for the sound of U.S. reconnaissance planes overhead. But none were flying. The airfields were still socked in.

Staff One was an elderly officer who had been a cadet with the general at West Point, and served with him in North Africa and in the invasion of Sicily. He was bald with a toothbrush mustache on a wise old owl's face. He still spoke with a Southwestern drawl and hand-rolled his cigarettes. He came into Buckley's shelter at dawn carrying a mess kit of hot food and a bottle half-full of Old Forester.

"Rise and shine, Buck. Old Balls Breaker is calling a meeting at ten to."

"Still snowing?" Buckley sat up and shivered, shook his head. "Can we hustle up any better maps?"

"I chewed out headquarters. They promised them to us last week. Here, dig into this, the stuff general's cook saved for you."

"First a bit of the booze to cut the morning slimes."

The whiskey helped to alert his bloodstream to shape up.

The whiskey and eggs—real eggs, not powdered—gave him a feeling life could be endured one more day. The two men had more of the Old Forester, and Buckley filled a pipe and lighted it. Staff One rolled a cigarette, licked the paper edge and pressed for a good, tight roll.

"Figured I'd stay out of the general's way till the meeting. He recites poetry." Clearly Staff One had had a few shots already.

"I've heard it. You been with him a long time?"

"Shit yes, since we were cadets at West Point. I don't know anything but army. I sometimes wonder what you fellas lived like. Take a rich Jew boy like yourself . . ."

Buckley said, "Ha ha," and punched Staff One in the ribs. "Wrong, I'm a wop . . . mostly. I'm not personally rich. The family runs a big bank, sure, but I was low dog, director of publicity when the big shootout began."

"Never roughed it?"

"Like hell I didn't. I ran away from college, palled around with the Broadway bootleg crowd in the twenties. Very fashionable playing palsy to the mob. Then me and another Guinea, Marco, ran gambling setups till some other gang didn't like it. I ran away to Mexico for a while. And then the Depression came in the thirties. Worked as a short-order cook, an oil-field roustabout till even that outfit folded. Then, then I came home . . . Jesus, what time is it?"

"Time for our meeting with the general."

"Any of that gargle left?"

"Just the heel. When you got back with your bank folk it must have been fancy."

"You'll retire on a good pension, with your medals and citations and you can write a book about the Balls Breaker."

"Hell, I ever do that he'd come at me with his mother-of-pearl–handled .45 and blow me away."

"He's got his bad side, I suppose."

"No, no, not a sweeter man ever lived, he's just a lovable crazy galoot and the greatest cavalry leader alive, even with tanks . . . They call him crazy; anyone is if you say what you mean."

Buckley took a brown envelope from inside his jacket. "Look, if action gets heavy and things go bad, *real* bad, mail this to my cousin Gregory, explaining, among other things, why I can't do an errand for him, and how much I love them all. Only send it on in case—"

"I know, if you get the deep six. Shit, Buck. I used to write 'em myself, every time things looked really bad. Now I save them for when we run out of toilet paper."

"Take it anyway."

The cold was worse outside, and snow was being blown about by the wind. The sentries were stamping their feet and saluting with mittens the size of boxing gloves. Watching his step, Buckley followed Staff One along the narrow trodden path of packed, soiled snow to the general's trailer.

Christ, Buck thought, truth is, I don't want to leave them. Penny, Gregory, Maude and Georgie, San Francisco, the bay full of white sails tacking in the wind. And the women, the good ones and the bad ones. The ones I was tender with and those I was a son of a bitch with . . . I don't want to die in a French forest.

"Buck, stamp your feet dry. The general keeps a neat trailer."

There were twelve of them in the trailer, and the electric heaters were on. The general was all smiles and beating the map table with his riding crop. His elation didn't penetrate to all members of the staff.

"Buck, what's with these goddamn maps?"

34

"A rider left with them from headquarters, but it's tricky riding in this snow."

The general nodded. "Well, there is always the old compass. Now let's go over the turns again, and no matter what weather, we keep moving. That clear?"

"Clear," said Staff Two, whose special job was to agree with the general. He was a lean, raw-boned man who never smiled.

The conference went on for half an hour, and Buckley drifted away to his own thoughts. He no longer felt he would be killed, but he didn't ask for the brown envelope back from Staff One. The general closed the meeting. Everyone left, leaving the Greatest Cavalry Leader in the World studying his maps.

Book Two

PASSION

Chapter Four

Stella Terry had never even had lunch with Gregory Fiore. Only dinner in his office off trays when some vital bank business had caused them to work late. This evening there was no meeting, no bank business, and Gregory Fiore had invited her to dinner at the Blue Fox. It had been a spur of the moment invitation on Gregory's part. They both had a hard day at the bank, and his son Georgie was going to appear in the city juvenile court the next day. Chauncey Cohn had borrowed one of the family cars without permission, and the boys had been stopped by the police.

As they ate their hors d'oeuvres—after martinis—in the elegant atmosphere of linen, silver and crystal, Stella studied the man she had known only during business hours for so many years. As usual, he seemed casual and at ease, even after two double martinis. But she had known him for too many years and through too many crises not to be aware that under all conditions he prided himself in always presenting a placid facade. Something was now annoying him. She thought it might be the war news or perhaps personal problems. Knowing he did have confidence in her and had asked her advice sometimes on small domestic matters, she would be discreet.

The martinis had been strong. She liked their glow. The maître d' offered them menus. "I can recommend the *sole Marguéry* with the mussels sauce and the herbed *gigot d'agneau*, Mr. Fiore."

"Thank you, Ernest. What would you like, Stella?"

She smiled, lifted one shoulder in doubt. "It *all* looks so impressive in print."

"Don't let it scare you . . . it's just food."

"All right. I've heard of roast duck with oranges; I'll give it a try." She was beginning to feel tipsy from the martinis.

"Of course," said the maître d'. "*Caneton aux oranges*, a good choice. Perhaps a *soupe verte* to start."

She declined that, and Gregory also ordered the duck.

"And the wine, sir?"

"Ernest, you know the Burgundy my grandfather liked."

"I do indeed." The waiter smiled and in a moment returned with the wine and two glasses.

Stella wasn't holding back. She ate with relish, nodding to the small talk, and felt as she sipped the wine that this was an event that might not happen again.

"I eat too much, Stella, with bankers or sportsmen, or just plain bores. At least you'll not ask me for inside market information."

"Wouldn't know what to do with it, Mr. Fiore." She wiped a corner of her mouth, hoping she hadn't smeared her lipstick.

"Call me Gregory, if you'd like. We're not at the damn bank."

Ernest suggested, "*Baba au rhum* or a liqueur?"

Stella, after the opening martinis and the heady wine, shook her head. She stared at the dessert menu. "I'll try *les fromages*—me who was raised on Jack cheese and Kraft."

"Good girl." Gregory winked at her.

Stella fanned her face with a hand. "I'm sorry Mr.—Gregory—I'm a bit tipsy." She put her elbows on the table.

Gregory grinned. She liked the way his eyes crinkled when he smiled. "Enjoying yourself, Stella? I am. The bank wives I know couldn't be fun even on a keg of gin. Stella, I'm wrapped up in too many goddamn things." She wondered if he wasn't a bit sloshed himself. He'd had two double martinis to start with and had drunk most of the Burgundy.

"This is relaxing." He wriggled his fingers. "The damn war news, it's a bit out of whack in the latest cables. I feel something's out of order in the advance into Germany. The news is too carefully worded."

Stella was feeling a tingling heat all over her body, and she wondered if the borrowed gown wasn't too tight and revealing. She flushed now and decided she wouldn't talk, just nod and look interested. She recalled the last time she had been in this condition and with whom; but she shook her head to shut out that memory and nodded as Gregory talked of his problems with his son Georgie.

"He's had some half-baked idea to change his education—wants to go away this summer and dig in Mexico, find some of those ugly pre-Columbian things, you know . . ."

She nodded, sat very still, a bit openmouthed, forming a little smile to cover up the fact that she had drunk more of the wine than she should have.

"Tomorrow I'm going down to Judge Melton's juvenile court to try and get Georgie and his friend Chauncey out of a jam. Chauncey—he's sixteen—had a learner's permit. Oh, the judge and I belong to the Bohemian Club, but I hate to ask favors."

She shook her head. "Of course not."

"Some ices, Stella?"

She said no, and managed to walk splendidly out of the Blue Fox. Gregory drove her to her small flat on Howard Street and saw her to the door of the three-story house.

"Oh, thank you, Gregory," she said. "It has been a really fine evening."

"Till tomorrow, Stella."

Yes, it had been a fine evening and she still felt a bit woozy. Then she lay on the bed, not fully undressing, just unzipping, unhooking somewhat; she grimaced at the ceiling where some rain stains were growing. Well, tomorrow was another day at the office.

The private chambers of Judge L. Amos Melton were quiet after the scurrying about in the hallways and courtrooms of young, small-time crime, hungry-looking lawyers and the shuffling around of papers and the checking of forms.

On his walls the judge collected Daumier prints mocking courts of justice. The judge was a well-fed man with skin weathered by golf, silver-rimmed glasses and large white teeth. He was a wise man whose view of mankind had not soured him completely. He sat back in his brown leather chair and looked up at Georgie, Chauncey Cohn and Gregory seated on the couch facing him.

"Kids take too many damn liberties these days, Mr. Fiore."

"I agree, Your Honor." He and the judge were at ease; the boys, grim-faced, glanced at each other sheepishly.

"Now the car was reported stolen, which is nonsense. Taking it without permission was bad enough, *very* bad." He thumped on his desktop with stubby fingers. "Driving on a learner's permit without a licensed driver along, bad bad. What do you think, Mr. Fiore?"

"They're very young boys, Your Honor. No one was hurt, thank God. They're really good boys, Judge. Of course, it's not for me to say what you should decide—to give them a police record or not." He avoided looking at the judge.

"Well," the judge said, looking at the two boys, "what do you have to say?"

Chauncey wet his lips, shuffled his feet. "Well, um . . ."

Georgie spoke up briskly. "Judge, you got us cold. We shouldn't have taken the car. I guess being sorry isn't enough."

Gregory spoke up. "Not by a long shot. Your Honor, if we could throw a bit of a scare into them, I would think—"

The judge stood up. He was taller than he appeared when seated. "There will be a guilty on a small misdemeanor charge. Goes on your records of course." He gave a puckish grin. "Maybe keep you out of the armed forces as undesirables—in peacetime. So, for six months, I'll put you both on probation to do social work during weekends, like grass cutting on county property, escorting old folks around at clinics. And we'll see what we can do about wiping out the records. How does that sit with you two?"

"Yes, sir! Fine, sir!" they both shouted.

"Get on your way."

After the boys left, Gregory thanked the judge.

"Oh, hell, Gregory. I took my father's old Model T when I was fourteen, started for the Black Hills to pan for gold." He turned thoughtful. "My father beat hell out of me later in the barn with a bit of mule harness. You think a good whacking is

43

what is missing in our modern treatment of the young?"

"I've heard arguments, Amos, on both sides."

"Who's to know, Greg. Say, that was a dandy-looking woman you were with the other night at the Blue Fox. You don't find ladies like that anymore."

Greg looked surprised.

"Like to see you getting about. Mourning too long turns a man dry and sour."

"That was my secretary, Stella Terry."

The judge pushed open the door into the courtroom, and turned. "Of course it was, G.F., *of course*."

A week later Gregory dined with Stella at a small Hungarian restaurant in Oakland, and three nights later they crossed the bay to the Blue Whale in Sausalito. Later, the bay blue-gray under a cloudy moon, he held her hand as if by casual accident, taking her home on the ferry. He kissed her there on the upper deck against a backdrop of red and green lights from a passing craft.

She had not objected, but said, "I don't think so, Greg."

"Don't think what?"

"I'm nearly forty, and now—"

"You've been hurt."

"Everybody has been some time, it's just—"

He put his hands up in mock surrender. "All right, but you still dine out with me. Goddamn it, Stella, I'm no teenager. I know *all* your answers. I know all the doubts in both of us. I'm not getting younger and I'm scared—alone. Yes, me, the big muckamuck of Pacific-Harvesters, scared to be on an express train called Time rushing me to an empty old age."

"It's, it's—" She turned away. "There's a lousy line in a

movie I once saw: 'We'll just be good friends.' It's not good enough." She was weeping, softly sobbing. Tiny waves beat on the hull of the ferry.

He said, "I'll buy it—good friends."

They had no problems working together at the bank. Both were experts at what they did. Things went smoothly, if a bit too formal.

Then came news of a confused battle in progress in the winter forests of the French-German border. Gregory spoke to her as he stood by the red stone fireplace in his office, filling his pipe.

"I'm going to St. Louis Tuesday to see about our outstanding loans. I want you to come with me."

She tapped her pencil against her dictation pad. "Yes, of course."

"You don't have to go."

"Want me to?"

"Oh, hell, Stella!" He snapped apart the stem of his pipe. "Of course, of course. But as—"

"I understand." She wanted to add, "But not just as a friend." "I'll make plane reservations and reserve hotel space."

He set aside the broken bits of the pipe, and came toward her. But she put out a restraining hand and pointed to the outer office. "Little pitchers have big ears."

He said, "I bet your grandfather said that."

Stella playfully stuck her tongue out at him, turned and went out of the office.

They spent four days in St. Louis in a suite in a small hotel on the edge of the city. They were very comfortable with each other in bed. Their emotions had been dormant too long. Everything was simple and easy between them. They were passionate lovers and did not want to think of the future. All that mattered now was the pleasure they took in each other. He also thought of Dr. Steinman's advice: "Moderation. Don't overdo it." Gregory felt moderation was for senile jaspers.

Chapter Five

Sergeant Ott had scrounged a woman's fur jacket, and he dozed by the bucket of embers, his face hot, his back freezing in spite of long johns, two sweaters and a leather vest, army-issue jacket and overcoat.

He looked over at Major Buckley Fiore—sleeping, scowling, twisting about a bit. Not a bad joe as officers went, and being his orderly was a good setup. Jake Ott was a wide Dutchman from a Pennsylvania farm, a twenty-year enlisted man.

It was still dark beneath the cover of a black velvet freezing atmosphere of mid-December when German storm troopers, under the glare of massed searchlights, came in solid formations of armor and battalions out of the Eifel forest. Swift in surprise, they at once overran the forward American positions in the Ardennes, the sharp rattle of heavy weapons and hand arms, and the thud of bombs echoing to the cries of the dying Americans. In the south and center, the corps of von Manteuffel's Fifth Panzer Army enveloped a thirty-mile front from Wiltz to Prüm and began to prepare to smother St. Vith and Bastogne. For the Americans, it became a horror as messages went back to their still sleeping generals, hastily awakened to climb into their pants and boots.

As for the Sixth Panzer Army, it was moving on a fifteen-mile front, tanks snorting blue smoke, coal-helmeted German troops breathing out white vapor—hasty messages coming through, as they crossed snowy ridges. General Dietrich was pressing all along the front from München and Melmédy. Heavy gunfire roared near the tank groups.

His sleep shattered, Buckley came awake in his hut to hear the banging bark of the hundreds of guns the Germans had positioned for rapidfire. The barrage was the biggest since D Day.

Buckley found himself staring openmouthed into his shaving mirror, which had fallen to the floor from the vibrations of the cannon fire. A new and more sinister sound was overhead, a chilling sound of almost flippant hatred. Staff One, tucking his shirt into his heavy ski pants, came in. "V-1s overhead, a hell of a lot going by, radio contact reports."

"Headed where?"

"Liège, Antwerp, or so they think by the direction."

"Must get through to headquarters. General Bradley's in Luxembourg. This catches us with our pants down. What's the weather?"

"Snow falling heavily to the north, and coming in fast all over the Ardennes. Means fighting a defensive pullback—if the generals have to regroup—doesn't it?" Buckley nodded. Staff One was a very good officer who never panicked. Not too much condescension. Unseen, V-2s were passing, speeding to put their high explosives into Antwerp.

He unfolded maps. "Holding anyplace?"

"No, from the few reports so far. What do you think? The Krauts gone crazy?"

In the general's trailer, a cold calm mood prevailed as the general lifted the phone, his fingers tracing a river line on a map. "Hello, get me headquarters in Luxembourg—highest priority. Position Dar Horse point five G." He turned to face Buckley. "As I see it—my cockeyed evaluation—it's the last big throw of the dice. Hitler plans to split the Allies, drive the British into the sea. He's wrong to—Hello. Give me Colonel Mantz—G.P. here, urgent, *urgent* . . . Yes, yes. The goddamn barrage is creeping closer. Get Brad to look at the maps and dig up my reports of the last two weeks." He was handed some fresh reports an orderly sergeant brought in. "They're out to seize the crossing on the Meuse." He looked at the reports. "Cross the river most likely between Liège and Huy . . . why not? I would if I were on their side. They'll push the Sixth Panzer to Antwerp on the right, and the Fifth Panzer, after they take Liège, bang through to Brussels. No, I don't say they will, I say that's what I read as their plan."

Staff Two came in, saluted.

"Any constructive evaluation on corps radio?"

"No, sir, not so far, General."

"I've got to stay in contact and keep communications open. Move out the nontechnical crews and the cooks, and—Hello, if what I said happens, you'll see a balls-up split between us and the English. Find out what Monty's reaction is . . . Yes, yes, that old bastard von Rundstedt is going on. *Es geht ums ganze*, which is, 'It's all or nothing.' Call me back after Brad is briefed."

Buckley was at the window as a shell fell nearby and exploded into a rose of fire and earth. Trees came crashing down. "It's beginning to snow, sir."

"I want him to fly his bomber crews!" shouted the general.

Staff One shook his head. "Lousy weather, we've not been able to send up any bomber planes."

"They'd better," said the general. He seemed elated at the sudden shift in the German pullbacks to this surprise attack. "The Germans are going to find their armor isn't going to move as fast as they planned. And snowdrifts are as bad as mud on tanks. They must cross the Meuse with no delay." He turned back to the maps. "Have to by the third day, before we can recover. And they'll have to depend on capturing our fuel dumps for gas."

A phone buzzed. Buckley picked it up. "Hello. Who? Yes, sir. Senior HQ, General Bradley."

He held out the phone to the general, who took it almost in jubilation. "Big doings, Brad—*big*!"

The day progressed badly; for the Americans, dank despair; and brilliantly for the Germans' wild optimism. The weather kept observation planes grounded. It was plain that the outposts, thinly held lines of Americans, had expected no attack and had gone down, been ground out and captured. The Germans, as they advanced, clearly expected the disruption and confusion of the Americans would grow. The heart of the enemy advance that day, maps showed, was toward the key road centers of St. Vith and Bastogne.

By noon the Germans were finding unexpected resistance in spots. Here and there, for all their confusion and snafus, the GIs were holding. Some disruption of regiments and crossroad positions was taking place and there were some troop movements. The beat-up unlucky Twenty-eighth Division, with great losses in the Hürtgen Forest battles and overloaded with raw replacements, was to be brought down from the north to Bastogne. Also, the Eighth Corps headquarters would have to make some hard decisions. The general remained calm, merely drinking coffee and breaking pencil points.

"Buck, we'll be moving north soon."

"I should hope so, sir."

"Get all the tanks to start warming up." The general turned to Staff Two. "And see all units gas up and load extra ammo."

Buckley went to see to his tank crews.

Sergeant Ott kept repeating, "A fuckup, a real fuckup," as Buckley's column of tanks began moving into a wall of snow.

Reports were regiments, badly bloodied, were holding some roads. The Germans couldn't get through according to some timetable. The enemy soldiers died in clumps of snow—like broken crows on wintry farm fields—snow here and there turned strawberry-colored.

The general suggested to headquarters that they order reinforcements from Luxembourg and from Reims. "They're up our ass like a bulldog!"

As for Buckley's tank crews, they spent the night in a great stone warehouse that smelled of wine vinegar. Wireless and phone crews were kept busy. Bleary-eyed, unshaven officers moved about with maps. Buckley, his long sheepskin coat belted tight, drank mugs of coffee. He waved off momentary distractions with a snarl.

Captain Swan had a large bruise on his forehead; he had fallen hard on the icy earth when his jeep was fired on by Germans dressed in American uniforms. In spite of the tension, the place took on a boisterous vitality smelling of dill pickles.

"Our Seventh Armored Division, sir, came rushing down from Aachen, picking up stragglers. Lots of battle-beaten sections."

"Where is it right now?" Buckley asked Captain Swan.

"It's supposed to be just outside St. Vith. It's fighting a pretty good withdrawal action."

"Don't tell the general that. He doesn't like the word *withdrawal*."

He got the general on the phone. "Buck? I think we're slowing them. HQ reports Dietrich's panzers got flogged by our Fifth Corps near the Ruhr dams. I hope it's true, not whistling in a graveyard. Christ, our rear organization is all haywire. We have no apparatus for withdrawal."

"What about our planes, sir?"

"No dice, ceiling still zero, and there are about two hundred Krauts from airdrops behind our lines disrupting communications. We need to annihilate them pronto!"

The general wanted every tank out on patrol. The twilight came too quickly. Dark and dank, the cold grew cruel and deadly. American confusion was still growing. At the end of the first day, the panzers had cut all the communications of the Twelfth Army group. Bradley's HQ in Luxembourg was cut off from control of his First and Ninth armies in the north. The Fifth Army was still under orders to attack the Ruhr river dams. The general wanted it to turn away to face the greater danger of the panzers. His request was refused by the senior HQ staff, which still did not realize the size and power of the German drive for a gigantic breakthrough. There was still no Allied concentration, rather a dispersion of interests.

Buckley went out into the cold with a jeep-and-recon convoy, moving warily to the sound of guns. He came back to the vinegar warehouse just before dawn, frozen, to drink brandy and coffee, sip overboiled soup and more brandy. He had a pretty good impression of German success, of what was shaping up. There were sounds of scuffling outside. A muddy squad of six soldiers in sheepskin jackets came in, and between them three other soldiers in topcoats. A lieutenant followed them, his face scarlet with frostbite.

The lieutenant saluted. "Sir, these men claim to be American soldiers separated from their units."

"Are they?" He glanced at the three stragglers.

"Papers look all right. They were in a jeep with the right markings, only . . ."

A blond soldier with buck teeth said, "We've been fighting, sir. Lost contact with our unit."

"Only what? What the hell's biting you, Lieutenant?"

"The uniforms, sir, are regular issue, but don't seem to have been issued at the same time by supply."

One of the three soldiers, smoking a cigarette, smiled. "We just picked up gear, it being so cold, what we needed from a depot that was burning, sir."

"Get rid of the cigarette," Buckley said.

The lieutenant handed Buckley a bit of paper. "I asked them to write out their names and serial numbers."

Walter Neyland	*23546-987*
Martin Brodie	*68523-890*
William A. Rome	*54692-684*

His eyes narrowed. He looked up from a close scrutiny of the writing. "The seven?"

"That's right, sir. No American draws a line halfway down the leg of the number seven."

A dark young soldier said, "I come from St. Louis. My folks are refugees and I enlisted to fight Hitler. I only had two years' schooling in St. Louis, so if the seven is . . ."

"Where did you go to school?" Buckley felt his gut rumble. "St. Louis."

"I never heard too many people call it anything but St. Louie, not St. Louis."

The dark soldier said calmly, only a grimace of mouth muscle active, "I am not too sure of proper usage yet." He fumbled at a pocket, got out a letter. "A letter from my girl, sir."

Buckley looked at the postmark. "Two months old. She doesn't write often, does she?"

He turned to the other two soldiers. "You, too, refugees?"

"No, sir," said the blond boy. "Born in Brentwood, California. Attended UCLA and played Little League baseball as a kid in Gilmore Stadium."

"And you?" he said, facing the soldier who had been smoking.

"New Brunswick, New Jersey. Apprentice carpenter at the Ford plant at Metuchen. I have my union card." He slapped his pockets, dug, handed over a crumpled green card. "It got wet. AF of L, Local Forty-three."

Self-confidence, but no audacity among them.

Buckley thought awhile. "That polack cook, Casmir, around? Go get him—the dentist from Hackensack."

He turned back to his map study. Hell, it wasn't his job, these soldiers. Let the MPs take them to Intelligence, if . . .

The soldiers, the squad guarding them, stared at each other.

After a moment, Sergeant Casmir came in, rubbing cold hands in a soiled kitchen apron. He gave Buckley a sloppy salute. He was wearing a heavy wool cap, a leather jacket and nonregulation boots. "Yes, sir. Trouble again with that molar?"

"Sergeant, as a knowledgeable dentist, I want you to look

into the mouths of these three soldiers. If there are fillings, can you tell if they're American work or European?"

"Don't see why not. Open up, you guys; you, wider."

The cook-dentist held a flashlight into each of their mouths. He turned and shook his head.

"Schlock stuff, sir. Aluminum fillings. Never could be ours. Jesus, I never saw that recommended, no real protection."

The three soldiers stiffened to attention, flung up their right arms, and all cried out, *"Heil, Hitler!"*

Buckley said, "Take them out under close guard." He motioned with a gloved hand. "Have them shot. We're moving out and we may be surrounded at any minute."

Buckley thought, In this war anyone can find himself victim or executioner. He felt ill, but firm. He himself could be dead in an hour.

Chapter Six

Buckley went up twice more in the scout plane to try to gauge some of the battle from the air. In hundreds of square miles on a front of over two hundred miles, the battles went on, and circling in wonder from above, flying to HQ in a Piper Cub, Buckley saw a bone-white ghostly world, broken here and there by burned-out areas where tanks still flamed, their crews consumed inside, roasting alive, stragglers rolling in the snow. Buckley saw the dead as blots along the roads and paths—Germans and Americans and some British, still bundled against a cold now turning their blood to ice, wool scarves fluttering in the wind. The scout plane flew low, vulnerable, unarmed, in weather too mucked up for fighters or bombers.

Here and there, in shattered woods, men still fired at one another.

* * *

When Buckley reported to HQ, he found General Bradley had come back from SHAEF and a conference with the supreme commander. Facing his staff, Bradley was anxious, settled in the conviction he was in trouble. Buckley was on one side of the big room in Luxembourg, trying to thaw out his freezing hands from the miserable trip in the jolting Piper scout plane.

"Well, you said we should be set for a counterattack."

"Yes, sir, it looks like we've got it," said Staff One. "More than a minor inconvenience."

"A counterattack . . . but, well, I'll be goddamned if I wanted one this big."

"It may be more than a counterattack, our general thinks. The size so far would indicate a full turning around in their plans. It's a hell of an offensive."

It was clear to Staff One the supreme commander did not yet believe it was a major offensive. But Bradley did. Yet still he insisted it was only a counterattack and a bog-down for the Germans. It was getting very late, and the men turned in for the night.

Buckley had just gone to sleep when Captain Spine shook him awake after midnight. Spine's frostbitten face was half-buried in a dog-pelt collar.

"Christsake, Spine, I need sleep . . ."

"Forget sleep. Orders are to move us north. The general says you are to organize the routes and work out the maps where we can rendezvous our tankers. It's all yours, Buck."

Buckley sat up and rumpled his hair, scratched his chest, yawned, then shivered. Spine handed him his sheepskin coat, which he put over his shoulders and stood up. He paced around his map table, stopping to make some minute analysis on the scrawled-upon maps.

"We move up from the Saar. Pronto."

"We're worried over deep snow and rate of speed. St. Vith and Bastogne may go at any moment," Spine said.

"The general can't fly six armored divisions north."

The general was having his boots polished by a black sergeant. Preparing to leave his trailer, he had his belts, straps and fancy weapons all in place. He had listened to Buckley and kept nodding while he replaced some new puppies in a padded basket on the trailer floor, while the bitch, with the litter tugging at her dugs, watched him with confidence. "Damn best batch of pups this ol' bitch ever threw. Go on, Buck, I'm listening."

"On paper, turning six divisions north with no confusion or loss of time is textbook dreaming. . . . Sir, if you don't object, I'd like to go with the Second Armored section. I trained with it."

"Find staff work superfluous, eh?"

A colonel came in and saluted. "General, all divisions report turning north on routes indicated."

The general looked up, grinned. "Good. We'll hit 'em right on their snouts. Buck is taking over the Second Tank Group. See he's filled in. Sure now, Buck, you don't want a champion Patton pup?"

For the next two days Buckley was extremely agitated. He rode in a command car over rutted trails and took a position in the lead tank of his column on a secondary road among ancient trees.

He gave orders. "Any tank that throws a tread or conks out, shove it aside. Keep going. Keep the columns taut and moving."

Suddenly, great blows of exploding shells on short fuses expanded, royal scarlet, rimmed in mourning black and containing steel fragments. Over all this rain of destruction, the heavy machine guns on the transports and wheeled cars were firing. The zong! zong! of bazookas had the mean perversity of a sound all their own. Like a turtle out of control, the tank slowly zigzagged toward the left just before its fuel, ammo and shells exploded in a great blasting roar.

Buckley, eyes to field glasses, found four German tanks ahead in a clearing waiting in ambush, and he radioed his right flanking columns to take shelter under some great oaks. He did not call for aid from the other two outer sections moving north. They must go on.

He ducked a blast of flying earth, leaves with a center of steel. He seemed unhurt. He had seen several direct blows of American shells pound against the enemy iron without entering.

A German tank became a column of fire as little black figures ran from it and a machine gun played its tune. The black figures lay still in the snow.

He felt something strike the tank, and his back teeth seemed to go loose for a moment. A fresh dent in the steel armor was just below him on the flank of his tank. Sergeant Ott's voice from below in the belly of the machine spoke up.

"Duck, sir. If they hit them chains we have piled up on the front of the crate, they'll come apart like buckshot."

"Keep rolling, Jake." Buckley's tank moved up to the action, and he became aware that one side of his face was singed and blistered.

The German armor was dying quickly as tank after tank hissed, roared and exploded. Buckley ducked down into the smell of the interior—a tank in battle, an engine grinding. When he again put his head out, the battle was coming to an end. An American column was coming up fast, firing; the group in the oak forest was in the open now, picking off surviving German armor. A cold rain began to fall, and then turned to a pelting sleet. The three surviving German tanks were taking evasive action, smashing against trees and barging over sapling and second growth. Buckley felt a serenity without smugness until his shoulder seemed on fire. He doubled up in pain.

The firing had died down and he panted, stood erect, climbed down, nearly falling by the side of the road. Captain Spine came riding up in a scout jeep, his helmet strap flapping as he leaped out and saluted, smiling.

"We did it! Sure did it, sir! Clobbered them! Got seventeen of their tanks conked."

"Prisoners?"

"Six wounded. Most aren't going to make it. Burns. Hey, sir, your face."

"Singed a bit."

"Get him to some medics," shouted Spine.

Sergeant Ott spat out a cigarette butt. "Christ, he's got a whole side of his head caved in."

Buckley was freezing. "Bury the dead. Get the wounded to the ambulances. Get me the general on the radio."

"He'll eat his heart out for missing this."

Buckley took three aspirin and drank big gulps of water from a canteen that the captain offered him. Only then did he become aware he had been badly wounded—had shattered a shoulder blade—and two men were holding him up and yelling, "Medic, medic!"

On the morning of December twenty-sixth, he was on the operating table, unconscious.

Chapter Seven

The problem of secret lovers, as it applied to Stella and Gregory, was that he wanted a great change and she was afraid of it. He wanted her to take over a fine, three-story old house with big bay windows overlooking the Embarcadero, but she did not want to leave her little flat.

As to the matter of their style of living, she would not move into the Fiore house on Nob Hill. If he stayed in her flat for a night or so, some of the Fiore servants whispered, and his daughter Maude, who often came up from Mills for weekends, would make sarcastic remarks to her father.

"Been tomcatting, dear old Dad?"

"Eat your Wheaties and respect your father."

"Aw, come on," said Maude, slathering marmalade on a toasted half of a bun, "I'm a big girl now. I'm eighteen and—"

"So?"

"So it's nearly 1945, all values are changing—you don't have to go sneaking away to some sleazy hotel with your secretary."

"Oh, shut up, Maude." He folded his *Wall Street Journal*, trying to speak naturally. Clearing his throat he said lightly, "There is nothing wrong in being with my secretary, only I don't know what you mean by tomcatting."

"Shacking up . . ."

He put down the *Journal,* picked up some Western Union messages from New York and Washington. "You should keep your mind, Maude, on that damn desperate battle going on. Christ, if Hitler breaks through to the Channel ports, it's snafu for a quick end to the war."

His daughter chewed thoughtfully. "You know what snafu is short for?"

"I have a fairly good idea."

"I'll tell you. It's—"

"You do"—he folded the paper, held it clublike over her head—"and I'll give you a beating Judge Melton favors we should deliver to our kids regularly, like the mail."

Maude giggled, licked marmalade off her fingers. "You're real funny, Dad. I only meant I think it's just great you're in there pitching again." She rose and hugged him. "Oh, I know, I know how much Mom meant to you, to us."

He patted her warm young shoulder. "Yes, it's been a bitch of a hard time for us."

"But now, Dad, we have to get along without her. I'm sorry if I riled you."

"I'm not riled and you're getting that damn marmalade on my shirt collar."

One kiss and Maude was gone—off for a morning ride with some friends to practice for a horse show.

Cody Hutton came in with a fresh pot of coffee. Gregory didn't approve of the modern way of making coffee at the table. Cody poured. "Nice to have someone to have breakfast with."

Gregory looked closely at Cody, but did not detect any ironic edge to the servant's remark.

"As you see it, sir, will Miss Terry be working with you on bank matters late this Friday and stay over?"

All Gregory managed to say was a crisp, "No!"

It had seemed like a fine idea for Stella to stay over at Cliff House. But Cliff House had too many servants, and Maude and Georgie came with their friends on weekends. So for a while, it had been the little flat. The neighbors got to know him, at least well enough to say good morning and exchange looks with one another.

Stella gave in to a better privacy, and they set up what she called "a sort of housekeeping in a sporting house built for two" in the house overlooking the Embarcadero. It solved their problems for a time. Stella could cook fairly simple dishes. He brought dusty bottles of wine, long kept in the cellar at Cliff House. They did foolish things with each other, talked in wild sentences; bathed, danced to their own versions of an older generation's music in the living room, a room to which Stella had added her books, including *Alice* in various editions and Jane Austen; large photos of Isadora Duncan, Greta Garbo and Eleanor Roosevelt hung in the bedroom. Gregory had gotten out of storage some Hudson River landscapes and a John Sloan 1910 New York roof scene.

Stella told herself to accept this happiness, this love; an understanding between two people harming no one, she told herself. But unlike Gregory, she felt a sliver of doubt wedge itself into her happiness. They invited no houseguests, gave no parties, still looked around them in the theater, or in restaurants, even when walking arm in arm in an art gallery.

The bank had to be attended to. The war in the Pacific was

becoming intense. The Germans were not being destroyed fast enough, and with the Battle of the Bulge in progress, the war was not, as Cody put it, "all fish and chips and your arse set safe in the butter tub."

When things had looked their worst, Gregory asked Stella to marry him. She said no.

Chapter Eight

The American air base outside Paris had earlier been German and before that, French. Major Buckley Fiore motioned his orderly, Sergeant Ott, to follow him past wrecks of planes, piles of discarded parts and mechanics eating sandwiches and drinking *vin ordinaire* out of bottles.

"Get me some damn kind of transport in to Paris."

Sergeant Ott gathered up Buckley's gear. Buckley still felt the jarring vibrations of the old army transport plane that had brought him to Paris from the hospital at Évreux. There were still some bits of shrapnel in his left shoulder and the streak of baldness, very thin on the left temple, showed where some steel fragment had grazed him; his hair would never cover the scar.

He was feeling a bit unsteady on the cement runway, but that passed as two planes took off to the left, past the limp wind sock. The war was still moving slowly, too slowly, but moving, and he was out of it at least for the moment.

Sergeant Ott came back with a British staff car. It was a

dun-colored Bentley, and the staff officer was a lean man, yellow with malaria.

"Happy to give you a lift, old man," he said to Buckley as they drove off past burned out storage areas and women picking over some acres of dumps. "Bad show, the Krauts jumping your chaps at the Bulge."

Buckley took a cigarette from the silver case offered to him. "You were there yourself at the end?"

"Yes, bloody work. Been to Paris before?"

"Before the war, lived here for a while," said Buckley. "I suppose the fountains on the Place de l'Opéra still flow and they still serve Pernods at the Dôme, if there is still a Dôme?"

"Jolly well is, and the sleazy *brasseries* on the rue de Fourcy. Haven't changed a bit—except the price has gone up."

"I'll keep that in mind."

He was happy to be dropped off at the Hôtel de Ville, where the Army had assigned him space. He checked into a room with one sloping wall and unwashed windows.

He looked at the address on the letter that Gregory had sent from Anita La Fiore and wondered if she was a fraud.

Buckley went to dinner at André's on the rue de l'Odéon and ordered the *terrine de canard*. He returned to the hotel and spent half an hour trying to get Henri Satie on a phone system that whizzed and hissed over a bad connection. But at last he had him on the hotel lobby line.

"So, Monsieur Fiore, you are in Paris. I have been alerted you were due."

"I am due. My cousin Gregory is very serious about reopening the Paris ranch of Pacific-Harvesters."

"So of course it has been explained to me." Satie's English was very good. "You are the 'head guy,' as they say in your country."

"Not yet. I've been wounded . . . nothing much. I'm due for discharge soon. Till then *you* are the head guy, okay?"

"Much okay. We must meet for the signing of certain permits. Paris is sinking under red tape and paperwork. Say the Chope du Nègre Café, noon tomorrow? They have a good menu and good *'le jazz,'* my son Paul Achille tells me."

There was more talk. Henri Satie, it seemed, like to test his English which was learned, he said, from watching American gangster films and an out-of-date series of language-lesson recordings.

Buckley slept well, the mattress and springs free of insect life. He breakfasted on croissants and jam from Sergeant Ott's carryall, coffee and pale blue French milk, after which, feeling at ease, he went out to walk to the rue St. Didier, where "Anita" lived.

He found the rue St. Didier an almost secret little street; he suspected that middle-class businessmen of no great income had little flats there for blowsy mistresses, and that shady characters housed themselves there. He laughed at these thoughts, his first full laughter since leaving the hospital. He realized that he had been dramatizing the street as if in a Simenon novel.

Twelve rue St. Didier was a narrow house, three stories high; its basement windows facing the street had pale pink flowers growing in Spam cans. The concierge was a neat tall woman with a baby in her arms.

She spoke in French. *"Vous cherchez Anita?"*

"That is right. Anita La Fiore."

The woman shifted the child to a more comfortable position. "If you came with bills or an overdue loan, she's gone. How much did she stick you for?"

"No, no. It's a family matter. Can you tell me where she may be?"

"All winter she has been staying at the Académie de l' Opéra. But I don't think she is there anymore—money problems, I'm sure."

"Do you have any idea where I can find her?"

"Ha! I hear she and some other students have formed a group and sing opera in the cafés on the rue Notre-Dame-des-Champs, Montparnasse, but who knows?"

Buckley held out some francs. "Thank you. Buy the baby a toy."

The woman thanked him as she took the money. "If you would care to see her room? Nothing is gone, she owes for six weeks. As soon as someone comes to rent, it all goes."

It was a small room, and he smelled bath powder. Several garments in need of cleaning were flung carelessly around. There was a banjo on a sofa covered with a red-figured blanket, several unframed posters of Paris streets in the rain, a small table with opera scores, an empty milk bottle growing mold, a seashell used as an ashtray, and some American paperback detective novels stashed under a small table. The room seemed to have a personality, an atmosphere hard to place, somewhat cloying. Some cheap cosmetic bottles were on a shelf over the washbasin. He found under the sofa a straw suitcase, in a corner an empty fishbowl. He noticed the concierge looking at him curiously. So he bid her farewell and left.

Once back in the street, Buckley felt there was something haunting about that room, as if he had found someone indecently exposed. It was a miserable place, not in any sense joyous, just a cheap room in Paris. This girl seemed somehow to suggest an angry personality. Could she possibly be his half-sister? He was in deep thought when he arrived at the Chope du Nègre Café.

Chapter Nine

Henri Satie explained as he and Buckley ate steaks and *salade de céleri*, "We French are too practical. So, to reopen the Paris branch of Pacific-Harvesters . . . the war is still on and the French are busy shooting their countrymen against stone walls for playing, as you say, 'footsie' with the Hitler people."

Henri Satie was short, quite bald, with a cheerful face betrayed by worried eyes and lines of suffering around his mouth. As he told Buckley, "I'm a survivor. But I am worried about my son Paul, an underground fighter, for the de Gaullists."

Buckley took out a filled pipe and lighted it with a silver lighter with the general's coat of arms and in Latin, *Palmam Qui Meruit Ferat*, which was given to him as a birthday present from the general.

"I'd like to discuss a personal matter with you. My cousin wants me to look into something, not a bank matter. It's about a girl who claims to be related to the family—she has been studying music during the occupation."

"I understand."

Buckley in the end had Satie write in a little notebook *Anita La Fiore, born in Mexico: citizen of France?* "If she is still in Paris, don't fear, we'll find her. I have connections. There are school listings, residential permits to sign for, forms to fill out. Passport checkings. In France even a permit to raise chickens is on the list."

They parted. Henri Satie lifted his melon bowler off his bald head in farewell and he went off, aided by a cane, a citizen of the Third Republic.

Buckley liked Satie, even though his loyalties most likely went to those whose money he took. Buckley would probably settle here soon and run the Paris office. He relighted his pipe while standing by a show window.

Two girls in short skirts above their knees and bare legs boldly advanced on him.

"'ello, Joe, what you know?"

"I know the sun's shining."

The taller one with a beauty spot near her mouth whispered to Buckley. "You come wif us, *hors de combat*, eh?"

"No, thank you."

"You want zigzag wif boat of us? What you like?" There followed detailed obscenities in English, French and even German.

He said, "No," and they moved on, arm in arm.

When he got back to the hotel, Buckley found a message waiting for him. The note was from Henri Satie. It was direct and short:

Anita La Fiore, displaced person. Passport 558-964-AJ (3). Entered France 1938; Origin Cadiz, Spain. Registered Opera Academy. Accused of stealing bed linen from Hotel Balzac— cleared, released. (Police files—YR 609.) Spent two weeks,

pneumonia, Clinique Chirurgicale Eugène Gibez, May 1942.
At present with a group of singers performing nightly at the
Café Le Bon Opéra in the rue Christine.

If one knows where to look, one can even find the devil.
Henri Satie.

Buckley decided to spend that night renewing his impressions of Paris. The bistros were sprucing up now that the war had moved east. There were even mangy Algerian rug peddlers and somehow a few poodles that had survived the hard years. He sat at the Coupole with *double fine à l'eau* and tried to recapture what it had been like when he was younger. Only a little of that nostalgia returned. Even if there were already *littérateurs* on the terrace hacking up Joyce and Proust, and little ferretlike men adding figures on small slips of paper.

Buckley asked for writing paper from the waiter and wrote out a cable to send off to his cousin Gregory about the bank branch, how it was progressing, and how Satie seemed to be the man who knew the process of getting things done. As for the personal matter of his father's claimed offspring, he added, he was proceeding to make contact.

On the rue Christine the military police walked in twos, with long batons in hand; the bistro owners all seemed to wear their caps low over one eye and smoked very short cigarettes. Buckley found the Bon Opéra Café between a hairdressing salon and a store for surplus auto parts.

Le Bon Opéra Café had no terrace and was reached by a series of steps going down under a small sign: LE BON OPÉRA EN SUITE. Buckley found himself in a low yet large room hung with faded crepe-paper ribbons of once bright colors. A dozen tables, a bar with no mirrors behind it and an atmosphere of naked light bulbs, chalky walls; tobacco fumes and stale wine that probably spilled and was never cleaned up. A broad-faced man carrying a tray of empty glasses pointed to a table. The place was fairly well filled with black soldiers speaking French, American military and middle-aged men in tieless shirts and dark jackets. The women, he noticed, were all very young. He thought they were probably music students.

He ordered a *bock* and *pommes frites*. A fat man with an Oliver Hardy face sat at a small upright piano and began to bang out some section of *Madama Butterfly*. There was no stage, just a platform. Two men and a girl appearing from behind a checked blue-and-red curtain began singing as the piano changed to *William Tell*.

Buckley studied the girl. She wore a pale blue underskirt topped by a dark red garment and a black blouse with puffed shoulders, the sleeves ending at the elbow. Her bare legs were hard and brown, banging on the platform in a sort of stationary dance step the group performed as they sang. Clearly the girl was the leader in the group. Her uncombed hair was inky black and curly, and she scratched her head as she twisted, whirled and rolled about. There was no spotlight, just two naked light bulbs partially covered by pale blue paper. Her dark eyes were rimmed with liner, and she had a long, well-made nose and a very mobile mouth.

The singing reached some very high notes and there was applause. As someone passed a hat from table to table, a drink was handed up to the fat man at the piano. The girl stood smiling, breathing in quick gasps, her bosom and torso inhaling, exhaling. Someone shouted at her. She shouted back, *"Couille!"* Back came, *"Sale con!"* Everyone laughed at the exchange.

The waiter set down a fresh beer in front of Buckley, and the girl held up her arms—someone made a coarse noise and the people hissed. The girl just said, *"Molle à la fesse,"* and went over to the piano and kissed the fat man's cheek, whispering in his ear. He began to play. Buckley thought it was something from *Tosca*. Two American military policemen with white helmets looked about them and left.

The girl was singing, standing very still, arms held to her side. She had a clear, powerful voice, and he tried to recall the plot of the damn opera; a stabbing and all that carrying on. In Italian of course.

There were more people now in the cellar, the smoke was thicker and the smell of wine, burning tobacco and urinal was stronger. Mostly the girl sang alone, sometimes backed up for short periods by two men . . . Buckley, when a very young man, had been in love with a former singer who became a teacher; they had been intimate, and so he learned to like good music.

That pleasure and understanding was coming back as he listened to the girl framed in tobacco smoke. He was fascinated by her. He had to find out whether she really was his half-sister. Or, maybe it was all just a carefully plotted setup. She knew how to be comfortable with an audience. She exuded genuine warmth, showing ease and spontaneity.

Chapter Ten

Buckley paid the waiter, who nodded, put away the francs and wiped the table with a gray napkin. He pointed to where Buckley could find Anita after the show.

The group bowed, the girl stood still, her neck and shoulders steady, her eyes wide open—she seemed to be looking right through the audience.

Buckley got up and moved past the tables to the back of the restaurant and looked down a dark staircase to the cellar. There was no door, just a narrow opening with a red and black curtain partially hanging in front of it. He slowly walked down the stairs. Beyond them he found a short passage and some wine bins with straw-covered bottles, and stopped at an open door marked LAVABO. He peeked past the door into a kitchen with an old woman chopping apart a chicken.

"La Anita?" he asked.

She pointed down the hall with the handle of the cleaver.

He came to a door, its green paint mostly chipped off with the chalk-marked name LA FIORE. Some private joker had added *"Entre quatre Yeux."* The door was partly open and he went in: a mirror, two chairs, one stool and a few stage costumes hung in a closet with no door. On a low table were the remains of a meal on a tray. When he entered the room, he stumbled over an old trenchcoat on the floor.

The door slowly opened behind him and the girl came in. She looked tired and her eyes were half-closed. When she saw him, she suddenly looked very tense and her eyes opened wide. Buckley thought of some theater star getting into character for an interview. She just stared at him directly. Buckley felt there was something bold yet slovenly about her. He felt very uncomfortable—an unwelcome intruder—and didn't know what to say to her.

"Got a cigarette?"

Buckly was slightly relieved by the broken silence. He just shook his head. She waved away the hope, and said softly, *"Merde."*

"My cousin, Gregory Fiore, has sent me to find you—it's about your letter." A bad beginning, he knew. She looked startled for a moment and then laughed unexpectedly.

"Got some money? I had to quit school, you know, because your dear cousin couldn't find the goodwill to send me the francs I needed."

"Do you expect he'll send money to any jane who claims to be a Fiore? And I've been fighting in the war. The only reason I'm here now is because I'm on sick leave."

"Very heroic." She waved an arm in the air. "So he sent you to find me." She hunted in an ashtray for a cigarette butt.

Buckley asked, "May I sit down?" She nodded. He felt himself sweating and unbuttoned his uniform coat. She sat down on the chair facing him, her elbows on the back of a chair, her exposed bare legs straddling it; he could only think of her in the gesture of a mounted rider.

"So, who are you in the Fiore family tree?"

"I'm Buckley Fiore, Fred's son, and possibly your half-brother. I'm only here to find out if you really are a Fiore—or, if you're just desperately in need of money."

"Do you believe me?" she said softly—Buckley thought, almost seductively.

"That will depend, of course." He took out his pipe and lighted it slowly. "Depends on how your evidence works out. You understand it has been a great surprise to the family."

"Oh, don't you worry. I have my birth certificate—even some personal letters between Fred and Inez. Give me a drag on your pipe—I am dying for the nicotine."

They both laughed awkwardly and he handed her the pipe. She puffed and exhaled and made a sour face. "*Mon Dieu!* Strong. Bad for the vocal box." She touched her throat. "I must be very careful." They talked for about an hour, and he sent out for a bottle of Meursault wine and a pack of French cigarettes. She was relaxed after two glasses of wine and her fourth cigarette—nostrils flaring, exhaling the smoke. Looking at Buckley with her large dark eyes, she wiped her mouth with the back of a hand. She began rambling. Buckley nodded politely, even when she spoke Spanish and French.

Her birth certificate, she explained, was in Mexico. "I was born in Mexico, in a city called Tamaulipas. My mother's name on the birth certificate is Lolita Angela Inez Hernandez Guzman Cortez Velarde. Naturally, no girl can drag all that around with her, huh? So when she began to sing, to dance, it became Inez Cortez. *El tiempo corre.* My father is listed just as Señor F. F. Place of residence, Los Angeles, U.S.A. I was raised by Aunt Concepción—not really my aunt, just somebody my mother paid to raise me. We were very poor, and I had very little education. I danced on holidays and fiestas, and sang in the cold church. Aunt Concepción was a cook, and we moved around a lot. We were living in a big run-down place in Ixtapalapa near Mexico City when my mother died—an alcoholic—and left Aunt Concepción very little money. So the two of us went to Spain, where I sang opera in cafés and danced in public for money—that's how my mother, Inez, had started. Sometimes I still find old cinema posters on walls with her picture on them—usually in a hot love scene with some handsome actor."

Buckley listened but made no comment. He was still very skeptical of Anita's story.

"In 1938 Aunt Concepción died and left me a little bag of money. I was sixteen. Taking the money left for me, I went to Paris where an old patron of music heard me sing and helped fund my studies at the Opera Academy." She winked at Buckley. "I'm almost through. So there I was, wild, but very vulnerable. I had already seen so many things—knew much of the world. But I'm sure you've had a rough time, in the war and all."

She lighted another cigarette. "I shouldn't smoke so much. I'm giving it up soon. Oh, studying opera at the Academy was fine. And Paris, if only the damn French would not be every damn place! You don't know, Major, what it is to be a starving artist with great talent, maybe even genius. It's a very special gift. But, like I said, I need money to live."

"And so you wrote to Gregory," he said, pouring the last of the Meursault into the two glasses. She was very tired now. Her head down, the flood of inky hair hanging loose and limp. She had talked for three hours. She stood up and stretched. She looked closely at Buckley, said she was very tired and lived around the corner. He offered to walk her home, but she said she'd rather walk by herself.

"Will you be around tomorrow?" she asked.

"Yes. Let's have lunch and we can talk some more, okay?"

"Tomorrow. Yes?" She laughed. "Okay—what a world. The place where you stay, they have a bathtub and hot water?"

"Yes, of course," Buckley replied.

"You have good American soap, Ivory, Camay, eh?"

"I am sure we can rustle some up. Come to my hotel at ten o'clock tomorrow morning.

She kissed him on the cheek and left him standing alone in her dressing room.

Buckley hailed a taxi, and the driver took the long way to his hotel. Buckley was too tired to raise a fuss. When he arrived at the hotel, he went right up to his room, washed and went right to bed. Something about Anita was bothering him. He felt strangely attracted to her and at the same time he was repelled by her. It took Buckley a long time to fall asleep, and he was awakened several times during the night by strange dreams that involved Anita. He woke up a ten A.M., quickly dressed, and ran down to the lobby to meet Anita. They had a hearty breakfast of eggs and bacon. The coffee was weak, and the waiter pointed out that Brazil was far away.

After breakfast they went up to Buckley's room, and Anita took her bath. When she came out with his gray robe on and her hair pulled back with a ribbon, she looked like a different person.

Buckley turned the radio on. Yes, there was still a war on, as the tiny battered radio announced that the Third Army protecting General Hodges's First Army flank was on the offensive and moving on the Siegfried Line. "Allied forces are on the north bank of the Ruhr River and crossing the German frontier."

"Oh, the war, *la grande illusion*!" she said, lying back on the bed, arms propped behind her head.

The radio answered, "The Ninetieth Division has taken the towns of Walchenhausen and Staubbach."

Buckley listened closely. "The French First Army has crossed the Colmar Canal. In the east, the First Belorussians have penetrated Germany in the region of Pomerania and—"

He snapped off the radio. "Enough bad news today."

They drank coffee, talked of Paris and its slow recovery. They talked, too, of Anita's vital papers in Mexico, and Buckley wondered if they really did exist. If things went well on the war fronts, he might be out of the service for good and he could go to Mexico to see if there was anything to substantiate her claim of being his father's daughter—or if he was just wasting his time.

It was a sunny day, and they walked through a few museums. He told her of his Uncle Ramon's great collection of art. Afterward they had lunch on the Boulevard St. Michel.

Buckley advanced her some money "against her claim," as he put it, so she could find a better place to live.

The next day he was busy with Henri Satie, meeting architects and painters. He and Henri together would start up the Paris branch of Pacific Harvesters. He and Anita had a late dinner at a musical society club.

The next day he had breakfast with Henri Satie, and they interviewed four top bank people to help with the initial management of the bank. For the next week he worked days and nights until things finally began falling into place and Henri could handle the operation himself in case Buckley had to go back to war.

There was a dance at the Allied Officers' Club. Anita managed to borrow an evening gown. They danced together, and several officers danced with her. A Polish officer remarked that she was well built and made obscene remarks to Buckley. Buckley just took Anita by the arm and they left. She had found a small apartment and, again, Buckley found himself "lending" her money to "pay the rent."

The war news was getting worse, and Buckley was asked to return to the war. Buckley informed Henri Satie. He had wished he could write back to Gregory with some positive information about Anita, but he really knew nothing—not until he could see her birth certificate and the letters himself. How long would this war last?

In two days, Major Buckley Fiore would once again have to report as staff officer to the U.S. Seventh Army facing the Oberhof-Drusenheim Line. Buckley did not tell Anita he was now in the war again until they got back to her room. When he told her, she seemed genuinely sad. "You know, I might never see you again," she said. "Why all this war, Buck? *Je ne sais pas.*"

He told her he would be back when the war was over, and if everything worked out and she really was his half-sister, they could go back to San Francisco together to live with Gregory.

He gave her a hug, kissed her and said goodbye.

Book Three

VANITY

Chapter Eleven

Dear Greg:

I've begun a letter to you several times, and always felt I had to clarify a bit more the situations on the two items I am following up for you. No, it is not my wounds; my shoulder is healed. I am back on the front and Henri Satie is heading up the branch of Pacific-Harvesters in Paris. It seems to be making rapid progress. I was on leave for three weeks, as you know, and I have made contact with the girl who calls herself Anita La Fiore. First of all, I'd say she is in her early twenties—a rather striking type. She does look much like Inez, and she has a great talent for opera. She did attend the school of opera she spoke about in her letter, and her singing voice is good. She is moody, rather unpredictable, and it's hard to get too many facts out of her. She claims her birth certificate and some letters of Inez and Fred's are locked away somewhere in Mexico. I can't tell if she's telling the truth or not.

I have talked to her almost daily, and all I can get from her is that the documentary proof exists in Mexico. She will not give me the address, but insists I go to Mexico with her, where she will then turn them over to me.

Anyway, I have left her with the promise that as soon as I get leave from the Army, I will go to Mexico with her. Let me just say that I am very doubtful she is the daughter of Fred and Inez, but until I see the papers, if they do exist, I'll try to keep my verdict open. It is not going to be easy, Henri Satie says, to prove any Mexican or Spanish document is genuine. Forgery, he insists, next to black marketing, is a European industry. Our embassy informs me a good section of U.S. passports presented are works of art and forgeries.

As for Henri Satie and the branch-bank matter, he will keep in touch with you and reserve any major decision for you.

As the French say: *En peu de mots*—in a few words, briefly—I don't know how much help I have been. I feel like when you used to take Penny and me to the magic show. I was enchanted and wanted to know how the lady was sawed in half, and yet also *not* wanting to know because an explanation would destroy the wonder of magic.

Your harassed cousin,
Buck

The lawyer, Jorgen Dalgaard, handed the letter back to Gregory across the desk. They were alone in Gregory's office, and the late-afternoon sun was slanting from low in the west, casting a golden wash over the paneled walls.

"What do you think, Joe?"

"Not much to go by. She sounds like trouble to me. We lawyers don't go for soft soap unless we're confusing a jury. Don't you catch on to her? She needs money, and for now, it's the easiest solution. Why the hell won't she tell him where her birth certificate is or those letters?" The lawyer rubbed his knuckles together, and said seriously, "Your cousin Buck is in a hell of a dilemma. He keeps trying to say in his letter she's a fake, that she isn't what she says she is, but there is also a sense that he's worried she *is* who she claims to be. Hope he's not falling in love with her."

"Why?"

"Don't you get it, G.F.? She'll tell him about her little scam, he'll forgive her—maybe even ask her to marry him. Wouldn't that be a perfect setup for a poor, starving talent!"

"Jesus Christ!" Gregory put a hand to his brow. "It never occurred to me that—"

"Sure. Whether she is or isn't a Fiore, she can get what she's after . . ."

Gregory lifted an eyebrow at the bad taste, but didn't seem surprised. "You're a clever, dirty old man."

The lawyer looked amused. "Here we have a soldier in Paris after a stay in a hospital, and meeting what is clearly some special chick. I'll have our investigators dig deeper into Fred Fiore and Inez's life, the claimed Mexican situation. Find out about this Aunt Concepción. See if these records exist and where." He leaned back in his chair and pursed his lips as some thoughts came to him. "There have been several false heirs and forged documents in court in the last twenty-five years. I'll look into them. Now, back to the Paris branch. You'll place Buck back as head of it?" He lifted up a dispatch case from the rug, opened it and took out a batch of papers. "The Paris branch setup so far seems to be in order. Satie is loyal, anyway. We'll have to lay out a bit of ready cash here and there to get the proper permits, certifications from a new government still in pretty vague shape. Satie can take care of that."

Gregory took the four-inch-thick batch of papers in their stiff blue binders and hefted them for weight in his hands. They all had to be reviewed and signed.

"Right away?"

"You know damn well you have to. It's important that you approve the reports point by point."

"Damn it, Joe—I have plans to take the kids camping next week. It's their Easter vacation. Guess I'll have to take them all with me. I'll have them signed and ready for you when I get back. Well, maybe I'll take Miss Terry along to help. There's a typewriter at the lodge, and she's a notary public." Gregory winked and smiled.

Jorgen Dalgaard sat expressionless and nodded. "Sounds perfect. I've reached the age where I wish sometimes, when drinking, I had some kids to take camping."

When the lawyer left, Gregory was flipping through the pile of papers and frowning. In the outer office, Stella Terry was sitting at her desk.

"Why do we have to go so early in the morning?" Georgie asked Cody Hutton as he packed his camp gear.

"A far way to go," said Cody as he closed one of Georgie's overloaded bags. Cody stood up. "Any more shit to lug along?"

Georgie's room at Cliff House had a punching bag, barbells on the floor, various movie posters salvaged from Uncle Fred's ventures into filmmaking, cases of books with colored illustrations. But Georgie was not much of a reader. He planned to go to Yale to study archaeology and dig up relics. He had a collection of Indian pottery, some Greek vase fragments, a replica of a Roman helmet and a Tang ceramic horse that had belonged to Uncle Ramon.

"I'll ride with you, Cody, in the station wagon."

"Your pal Chauncey coming with us?"

"Not today. He's joining us later up at the lodge. He's

spending some time with his parents. I know he'll get bored real fast. The Pineridge crowd from L.A. just sit around on their duffs boozing it up and dressing up for dinner." Georgie faked a yawn. "Chaunce says the waitresses are all Indian girls, and easy to lay."

"Christ!" Cody kicked aside some tennis rackets in presses. "Watch your mouth. If your father heard you, he'd wallop you!"

Below on the big veranda, Stella waited, wondering if she was overdressed for camping. She'd bought blue jeans, a suede fawn-colored jacket and new boots just for the trip. She was anxious. This was the first time she would spend time with Maude and Georgie.

They took two cars—the black Lincoln for Gregory, Maude and Stella Terry, and the station wagon for Georgie and Cody. Maude, who had come up from Mills College for the Easter break, talked to Stella, who at once felt comfortable.

For a while they drove, the station wagon trailing behind them. They drove by the ocean, then past vineyards full of crimson clusters of grapes, past umber hills and pastures. They drove along paved roads to country pikes of crusted stone and tar, and at last were on a dirt track among tall, dark trees. Maude fell asleep and Stella, in the front seat, rested her head on Gregory's shoulder. Finally, they pulled into the Fiore lodge, set on a lake in the middle of several thousand acres of preserved wilderness, surrounded by enormous pine trees and mountain oak. Maude and Stella got out of the car first. Maude grabbed Stella by the hand and excitedly pulled her toward the lake, with Georgie following close behind.

Maude asked, "You a Catholic, Stella?"

"No, a nonpracticing Baptist."

Cody unloaded the cars, and Gregory unlocked the door to

the lodge. The lodge, like a great humpback whale, stood with its gables under ancient trees, verandas on three sides and two picture windows with heavy shutters. Stella, Georgie and Maude came back, a little out of breath. Maude remarked how beautiful the lodge was. The stone fireplaces, one at each end, could have barbecued a whole ox. Stella was impressed by this surviving grandeur in the wilderness, built of rough timbers and polished boards by George Fiore at the turn of the century.

Chapter Twelve

Maude had named the lodge Liberty Hall that season. She had taken her first baby steps there. She and Georgie wandered off to one of their favorite clearings. They both lay down in the shade of a bit of surviving wall, chewing on grass stems, hands behind their heads, wearing large straw hats.

Maude yawned, stretched, rolled over and punched her brother in the ribs. "What do you think of Stella?"

"She's all right, I guess. Yeah, she's okay."

"I mean her and Dad, you *know*."

"Know what?"

"What?" Maude smacked him with her straw hat. "They're sleeping together."

Georgie sat up, pushed his hat back over his forehead. "You mean, they . . . Pop—screwing?"

"That's a vulgar way to put it. I think it's wonderful, don't you? At their age?"

"Hey, they're not in wheelchairs yet. But I just figured Stella was helping out with those bank documents."

"Boy, are you dumb." She looked at her brother closer. "What do you and Chauncey talk about?"

"Stuff."

"What kinda stuff?"

"Boy's stuff—football pool percentages, stealing cars."

"What about girls? Petting? Necking? Scoring?"

He looked at his sister with distaste. "That's disgusting. It's none of your damn business, Maude."

She tickled his cheek with a long blade of grass. "You know, Georgie, you're full of shit."

He stood up. "Girls with the hots think they're so goddamn smart, don't they?"

"Smarter than dirty-minded prep school kids. Tell you what, Georgie. When your chum Chauncey comes, I'm going to seduce him . . . That's right. I'll spell it out for you: S–E–D–U–C–E."

Georgie tapped his head with a finger. "You girls are all crazy."

"I'm going to S–C–R–E–W him, brother Georgie—and don't you doubt it."

All he could say was, "Ha ha!"

Maude, as Georgie started walking back to the lodge, stood, legs apart, waving her straw hat in great swooping circles over her head. "And Dad and Stella are D–O–I–N–G–I–T !"

It was a small victory for Maude that Georgie had not had the last word. He just walked away through the tall grass, never looking back.

It was a lovely day, and Maude went to a small stream nearby that ran into a fishing pond. Barefooted, she splashed about in the stream, spun around to look at the blue sky with its drifts of little wool clouds, and noticed a pair of hawks circling above some dead pines. Ahead, she saw the rise of the fields and the berry patches. She was feeling unusually excited today. She felt womanhood rushing her: too much book reading and too many sessions with the girls at Mills talking of life, men and passion had made her itchy. She felt she was missing wonderful experiences other girls her age were having. Soon she would graduate from Mills, and then what? Marriage? Children? She felt dizzy and she flung herself down into the brook, rolling over and over, sat up, sprayed water from her mouth like a fountain and laughed loudly, disturbing the circling hawks . . .

Stella and Greg decided to go fishing and took the canoe up the lake. Cody had packed a picnic lunch for them. The spot Gregory picked was sheltered by overhanging trees that made patterned shadows of the deep emerald pools. On the pebbled bottom of the lake, crawfish scuttled about; above them the trout took noonday naps. On the surface, skating water bugs with long legs raced about to warn of intruders. They were on a section of sandy beach in a remote cove. Here Stella had laid out their picnic on a big blanket, and Gregory had submerged the wine bottles in the shallows of the lake to cool.

Insects buzzed nearby. The soft lap of the lake against the beached canoe and the fluttering aspen leaves fascinated Stella. She turned to Greg, picked up a chunk of cheese and said, "For all your savvy as a hard-nosed banker, you're a damn romantic, Greg. I love you. You love me. Beyond that, I don't know where that'll take us."

"Come on, doesn't this lake, the sky, the smell of the food give you a feeling that you should trust life to take you wherever you should be?"

"I suppose." She was kissing him and they locked in an embrace. A soft wind rippled the water's surface.

He began to unbutton her blouse. She held his fingers firmly. "No hurry, darling. Let's just breathe in this place, absorb it. We're alone now. Just two foolish middle-aged folks."

"Look, if it is permitted for some to be young fools, why not for those who have the wisdom of years behind them? Didn't someone once say youth is wasted on the wrong people?"

"I'll remember that. Hey, let's have a swim before lunch," she said coyly.

He looked at her closely, and was surprised she had a daring sense of adventure. He was aware there was a secret core to her that he would most likely never reach. Gregory supposed, as so many men did, that it was impossible to know women fully. That they were "creatures existing in part on different planes," or so Joe Dalgaard had said.

How cynical, he decided, as a flight of wild doves passed and Stella slipped out of her clothes. He said, "No bathing suit?"

"No way, we don't need a damned thing here." She shouted at him—daring him to undress and jump in with her. Before Gregory knew it, he was standing naked, facing Stella. They were well made, put together solidly—middle age had not misshaped them. Gregory had a bit of a paunch, and Stella's large, well-formed breasts sagged a little. But, to each other, as they stood there, they felt young again. Gregory looked forward to good, passionate lovemaking. Attainment, not restraint, was their goal here in the private wilderness.

They dived into the lake and swam far out. She was more skilled than he was in the water, and had a grace of form he lacked. He had a brute power and was a bit awkward in his movements. They touched, kissed and thrashed about for some time. When they finally came out, their skin and hair streaming, they stood in a sunny patch to dry, toweling each other, kissing, reaching, hugging and saying outrageous things to each other. Stella laughed and slapped Greg's limbs and torso till Gregory grabbed her and pulled her down on the blanket, where they made love like never before.

Engaged in body play together with skillful care and ease, they were in no hurry until their climaxes came in that delightful struggle for breath, their hearts pounding until they lay silently together, fingers entwined. Both of them dozed off. When they woke up, they ate hungrily, teeth flashing, smiling at each other, tearing into the tender chicken sections and fish, biting with strong jaws into the crisp French bread. "I'm starved!" she said, brushing crumbs from his mouth, then pressing her greasy mouth to his. Drinking their wine they laughed a great deal and some spilled from Stella's mouth; it ran down between her breasts to her navel and then to her pubic area.

"Did the earth shake?" she asked.

"Did the trees sway? Let's go to the sleeping bag."

They slept, until shadows turned from blue to deep plum color, and the afternoon insects began to come over from across the lake. When they woke up, it was late and they quickly dressed and packed the canoe. They got back to the lodge to hear that President Roosevelt had died suddenly. The shortwave radio at the lodge had picked up the news sent out by a forest-ranger station at Red Bluff.

"It doesn't seem right," said Maude. "I mean, he was entitled to be there at the end of the war. He did so much for us."

"He lived too hard," said Gregory. "He looked exhausted at Yalta."

Georgie, who was at the shortwave set, lifted an earphone off his head. "Why did all the kids' folks at school hate him?"

"Because, damn them," said Stella, "he saved their dads' hides in the thirties and later rubbed their faces in it."

Gregory was writing on a yellow piece of paper. "I want you to send this shortwave, Georgie, to the bank." He adjusted his glasses and moved to a better light to read what he had written.

> Urgent: Check all our flags are at half mast. Take space in S.F. papers for the following: Quote: With the rest of the Free (capital F) World (capital W) Pacific-Harvesters Bank and its branches around the world mourn the passing of our heroic President and Commander-in-Chief. Not only do we Americans owe him honor, but the entire world of nations whose cause for freedom he took up know this was a man of the greatest merit and compassion, who directed the finest of our efforts. End quote. Add to my message the simple logo of the bank, and in small type "Gregory Fiore, President." Add also names of the Board. G. F. The Lodge.

It was a gloomy night at the lodge. Cody got drunk in the old coach house. Maude wrote in her diary. Gregory and Stella did not make love after they went to bed.

Chapter Thirteen

They were seated at dinner at the lodge, still half-numb with shock. With time, the greatness of the dead leader would become clearer, as would his faults, Gregory insisted.

"Damn it, Stella," Gregory said, taking the crackling roast from Cody's hands. "He was a man, had a man's faults, but he saved the game when Hoover fumbled the ball."

"Rules of the game, eh?" Maude grinned. "He died with his girlfriend, very cozy. Oh, hell!" She looked from her father to Stella, and she banged a fork against her plate. "I'm sorry."

"Greg, you going to the services and ceremonies at the Capitol?" Stella asked.

Gregory began to carve the roast. "I suppose. I'll wait for a response from the bank—see if I've been invited."

Maude, embarrassed about her remark about F.D.R.'s special woman friend, hunted for a safe topic for table talk.

"Old George hated the man," Georgie remarked.

"Only his banking-laws idea. He cast his vote for him, even

went to Washington for the inauguration. His final trip away from Cliff House."

Gregory took a sip of wine. He didn't say much at all that evening. Stella excused herself and went upstairs to the bedroom. Cody began to collect the plates. After dinner, Gregory, Maude and Georgie sat around the radio, which blasted noisy tributes and ritual music. The sense of loss, Gregory felt, was becoming a bit too cloying. The media, as usual, was touting itself by hysterical prose. The next day, Gregory would probably have to leave—he wished he wouldn't be invited to the Capitol for the long-winded ceremonies. But it would be poor public relations not to go, and he did have to get the papers settled for the Paris branch of Pacific-Harvesters.

As Gregory waited for Cody to bring the Lincoln around to the front of the lodge the next evening, he stood with Stella. They held each other closely. She had offered to go back with him, but he said he really had to get some work done and he would see her at the end of the week when everything settled down. The death seemed to have made Gregory and Stella more vulnerable and aware of their mortality.

She said in a low voice, "Why do people get sentimental at twilight?"

The big car came crunching on the gravel. "Goodbye, my dear," said Gregory.

When the Lincoln had gone down the rutted road, Stella stood looking up at the sky, wondering why happiness was so often bordered by sad little thoughts. Here she was, a mature woman, well-loved, and for the first time in her life someone took care of her. She was working for the man she loved. She flushed as the twilight deepened. She walked slowly up the rough stone steps to the big veranda. No, she had no regrets. Even the thought of marriage didn't scare her right now.

Maude came out with two heaping bowls of ice cream. "Which do you want? Chocolate or strawberry?"

"Chocolate, thanks."

"Look, Stella, I want to say I'm sorry I was such a shit at dinner yesterday."

"Just a little one," Stella laughed, and put her arm around Maude.

They ate their ice cream in silence, and after a while, they both turned in for the night. Cody and Georgie had already gone to bed.

The next morning there was a squall on the lake, and after it passed, Georgie, standing on the veranda, sighted a kayak far out and ran to the shore wondering what damn fool had been out in such weather. A young man waved a paddle from the kayak, and as it drew nearer Georgie saw it was his friend, Chauncey Cohn.

"You are crazy!" he shouted at Chauncey, who was drenched and shivering.

Chauncey shouted back, "You're so friggin' right!" He could hardly paddle anymore, and Georgie was preparing to push the rowboat into the water to pull him in. But Chauncey came slowly up to the little dock and sat in the kayak, wet, panting and trying to smile. "Christ, whoever expected something mean like that to blow up from nowhere."

"The lake does that sometimes. Come on, you're shivering." He helped his friend out of the kayak and put an arm around the shaking figure. "You need some hot soup, and a good kick in the ass."

"It was a close one." Teeth chattering, Chauncey managed a smile. "I mean, started a beaut of a day . . . I wanted to get away from Pineridge. Some of those rich pricks were actually celebrating the death of F.D.R. I mean it, chum—singing! Would you believe it?"

97

"Stop talking . . . just hold to me, it's just up the path."

Once in the lodge kitchen, Cody poured some hot soup into a big bowl. Chauncey sipped, shivering under the two blankets Cody had wrapped around him. Maude thought he looked very handsome, his dark hair in wet curls framing his tanned high forehead—a sort of Hebrew Lord Byron, she thought. His tall body and long, muscled legs suggested to her a virility that her brother Georgie still lacked. Chauncey, only a year older than Georgie, was already a man.

"When the storm hit, there was nothing left to do but paddle," he said, gulping the soup. "But these goddamn big waves—I couldn't see shore anywhere. Funny, I was so busy paddling I forgot to be scared."

Cody held out a flask of brandy. "Take a sip of this. You don't go across Crystal Lake in this kind of weather if you still got all your marbles. Why did you do it?"

"Oh." He choked on a sip of brandy and waved off the flask. "Oh, it was calm when I crossed over from the upper lake. I carried the kayak across a strip of rough water. It looked like a cinch, no sweat. Then *zam*, the wind and waves suddenly went nuts. Just nuts. Never seen anything like it . . ."

Stella came in with an extra blanket. "Georgie, get his wet duds off him and get him into bed. We don't want him to catch pneumonia."

"No, we sure don't," said Maude.

Chauncey said, "My gear and carryall are inside the kayak."

Georgie led his friend upstairs while Cody went out to fetch Chauncey's gear and secure the kayak to the dock.

They were all a bit charged up by the event. They all momentarily forgot about the death of the president.

Chauncey recovered swiftly after a night's solid sleep. He

rather enjoyed the attention he created, sitting on the veranda in T-shirt and shorts, taking secret pride in his adventure. "I'd like to find a couple of big turtles for the garden I'm making. Maybe some old tree stumps or rocks."

Maude said, "There's an old trapper's cabin, all rotting out. Just the sort of place turtles like to hide."

"I want two turtles big as saucers. What do you say, Georgie? We go sack and nab a few?"

"Damn the turtles. I'm digging at the old mission site, and I think I saw signs of a big stone altar. Why don't you come with me?"

Chauncey thought he'd rather stalk turtles. So he and Maude skipped off together down the path to the old trapper's cabin. Georgie was in a bad mood. He said to Cody, "To hell with friendship between men when there's a girl around." He went off by himself to the mission site. Stella rose late, and Cody warmed a cup of coffee for her. They sat together on the veranda, enjoying the peace and quiet after the kids were gone.

Chapter Fourteen

"We haven't seen a turtle yet," Chauncey remarked, easing the backpack on his shoulders.

"There's a glade by a little pool where scads of turtles come out to sun themselves. Come on."

Chauncey was a bit irked. The way was wild and the trail was almost covered by underbrush. But the girl seemed to know her way and, in slacks, pullover and boots, didn't seem to mind the insects. Chauncey swatted at his neck where a mosquito was attacking him. "How much further?" He had always prided himself on his woodmanship, but Maude seemed to have much more knowledge than he and it was irritating him.

"There it is," said Maude, pointing out the old trapper's cabin.

"What's left of it."

They stood staring at two decaying log walls, a broken roof, slabs of bark, a door fallen off its rotted hinges. The glade, however, was pleasant, and a little breeze coming from a cleft between two hills kept off the insects.

Chauncey cheered up and gave Maude credit for being a trailbreaker. Maude suggested they rest and have some cold lemonade from the thermos jug she brought along. They sat down, stretched their legs and sipped. They talked about Indian warriors, since Chauncey had told her he was an expert in Indian lore. Maude asked if Indian sex life in any way compared to that of white culture, and Chauncey admitted he had no idea about that.

"Are you a naturalist, Chaunce?" she asked flirtatiously.

"Sure, I guess so."

"Well, you'd think being a naturalist, Chaunce, you'd find sex part of nature, wouldn't you?"

Chauncey rubbed an insect bite on his naked leg. "I don't know, Maude. What are you getting at?"

"It's grand we're freer, franker, don't you think?"

He admitted to that fact, and Maude said, "I suppose you've made love to lots of girls."

He humbly said he didn't like to brag.

"Oh, come on, Chaunce, we're grown up. It's 1945. You're probably experienced in that kind of thing."

"Thing?"

"Copulating, fornication, sex—well, what would you call it?"

He swallowed some lemonade and coughed. "I'm a gentleman—I don't talk about it."

"I can see your viewpoint on gossip." She lay down on the soft, dry grass. "Look, I want you to fuck me."

"What!" He coughed and sprayed lemonade into the air and looked away. "That's a word I don't think any nice girl should use."

"Words, words! I'm normal, you're normal. It's what nature demands of people, full steam ahead."

She was slipping out of her slacks and pulled her sweater off over her head. "Shuck 'em, Chaunce, shuck 'em."

"It doesn't, well, seem right, you being my best friend's sister."

She pressed her small firm breasts close to him. "You haven't felt this about all the other girls you've screwed, have you? You're a real cocksman, Georgie told me—say, you're not just making it up, pronging all those girls," she teased.

"Well, no. But we came to find turtles and—I'm not prepared, sorry."

"Don't worry, I am." She dug into a bag she had been carrying over her shoulder and brought out a tin of Trojan condoms, a towel and a bar of Palmolive soap. "Everything we'll need. It's my first time, you understand. Did I forget anything?"

"No, damn it, Maude—NO! There's, there's, well, I don't wind it up like an alarm clock."

She knelt down over him and put her hand on his crotch. "The hell with talk, I'm ready. Can't get it up? Let me help."

He pulled away in panic, turned red and tried to get up. She rolled against him and put her arms around him. "This, frankly, is not the way I expected it to be. No ecstasy, passion, all senses gone wild," she said, disappointed with her experience.

She was probing his crotch again as he struggled to free himself. "Oh, my. It's a darling erection, nothing to be ashamed of." He felt her at his zipper and failed to fight off her fingers, and soon she had him in her grasp. He could not unlock her fingers.

"Look, look, don't be crazy!"

"Kiss me, kiss me, Chauncey."

But he thrashed his head away as she moaned. "Listen, Chaunce, is it against your religion? Tell me, Jews, they don't permit deflowering a virgin?"

"It's not that, but you're Georgie's sister." He turned the other way, curled up into a ball, head on his chest, legs drawn up with his hands locked around his knees. He wanted to disappear somewhere and cry.

She stood up, naked and outraged, and shook her head furiously. "You poor lying bastard. You've never done anything but beat your meat, if that. You're scared. You know what you are, sweetie boy? Whatever you are, you're not a man."

She turned and went past him to the spring and went for a swim. She dipped herself twice, cooling her flushed skin, but her outrage had not abated. She felt neither ashamed nor humiliated.

Chauncey lay very still, not making a sound. He could feel his heart pounding. He wanted to die here. No, he just wanted to be far away. Better still, he wished it was all a bad dream. He was humiliated—no longer clever, worldly Chauncey Cohn. He reached for the zipper and quickly zipped himself up, got up and ran for the cover of the woods to get away from Maude. He headed straight to the boat dock where he sat for some time, then untied his kayak and the double-bladed oar and sadly paddled off into the lake.

Maude returned to the lodge late and, when asked where Chauncey was, she explained he had decided to stay and catch some turtles at night, claiming that's when they came out to feed. But when Georgie realized that the kayak was gone, he asked his sister.

"You and Chaunce get into any kind of hassle?"

"Good Lord, why should we? He was kind of moody all day, sort of spooked by the old cabin."

"Chaunce gets hurt easy. He's very sensitive, Maude."

Maude sighed. "There weren't any turtles, those dumb critters. Maybe they set off a whacky mood."

Cody looked from sister to brother and said sternly, "Let's hope tonight he's got a smooth lake to cross."

Maude went to bed early that night while Stella, Cody and Georgie stayed up. They were all thinking about Chauncey and hoping he was all right. Gregory called on shortwave radio and Stella answered. Georgie managed to fix the connection so they could have a conversation.

"How's Washington? I miss you."

"Mad. You'd think there was a war on, Stella. How you holding up?"

"Fine. We're all fine."

"You wouldn't believe this town. Everybody plugging their interests, their section, their power position, circling their wagons, firing away."

After that there was static, and the conversation was not too satisfactory. Stella hung up the receiver. In a few days, she could be with Gregory again.

They did hear news of Chauncey Cohn. Chauncey had made contact with a shortwave operator at Pineridge. He said not to worry and that he was home safe. When Georgie asked him why he left, he replied that he never could be in one place for more than a couple of days. He just got itchy.

After Georgie hung up, they all went to bed. Everyone slept soundly, except Maude.

Chapter Fifteen

Washington did not slacken its pace, even with its great leader dead. Clearly, as the headlines claimed, the war in Europe was drawing to a close. Gregory, in his hotel room, listened to the news of the Russian armies moving deeper into Germany, and decided to visit Buck's sister, Penny, who lived in Georgetown.

As his taxi let him off in front of the rebuilt two-story brick colonial house in Georgetown, Gregory thought how long it had been—over a year—since he'd seen Penny. She had become one of the top Washington reporters, and her husband, Harry Rodman, was a famous songwriter. Penny had been among the first to do a good job of converting a mid-nineteenth-century wreck into a fairly charming house.

A maid let Gregory in, and Penny met him in the low-ceiling living room and gave him a big hug.

"You look fit, Penny." They kissed each other and held hands for a moment. Each noticed how much older the other had gotten.

"Getting on, Greg, getting on. Be an old hen soon." She still had a good color, a fine figure. She had the Fiore nose like her brother Buckley. And, yes, she had hardened, Gregory felt. There was a kind of smooth cosmetic surface, a fashionable polish. No flashiness, just a gold bracelet and a flat jade pendant around her neck. She had an original sense of style and grace.

"P-H running smoothly? Can I get you a drink?"

"I've been boozing Washington style; how about just white wine?"

She gestured to the maid. "Scotch for me, white wine for Mr. Fiore."

Gregory felt very comfortable with Penny. It was cozy to sit with her. They had grown up together, shared in some of the high jinks of the twenties.

"How's Harry?"

"He's out of town for a few days—keeping busy, as usual. You know, Greg, I miss not having children—not that Harry isn't great company when he's around. I miss him, but I manage to keep busy. Women's Services, goosing the White House to keep its bombers away from art-treasure cities. Kill people—save the Rembrandts! It's crazy. Heard from Bucky?"

"Back in harness. I was hoping he'd do some investigating for me. For all of us, while in Paris. Listen, Penny, you know your father was a man to take his pleasures here and there."

"That's my Pop."

"Ever heard anything about a child?"

"Dad could have spawned half a dozen little bastards. If so, some of them or their mommies would have stepped forward before now, asking for a payoff. Nobody has, as far as I know."

"There's a girl who was in Paris during the occupation who

claims to be your half-sister. Calls herself Anita La Fiore."

Penny was amused. She reached for a cigarette from a glass box. "Where does 'La' come from?" She lighted her cigarette, inhaled and exhaled. "I like this broad's style. La Fiore. Something to stir up old bones in closets. Who's the mommy?"

"Inez Cortez, she claims."

"Ah, the mysterious Inez. Very logical, Greg. And why not? They certainly were a pair of noisy passion flowers. Fighting in private, yelling in public. They were a regular three-ring circus."

Greg put down his wineglass. "She claims she was born in 1922. Truth is, he was getting senile, Penny. Anyway, about Anita, we've seen no documented proof of birth yet. Buck is going to follow it up as soon as he can. He's going to run our bank office in Paris—if this war ever ends."

Penny beat out her cigarette in a small ashtray and went to stand by the fireplace. "Bucky should marry, have some kids. I feel Harry and I let Old George down. Jesus, Greg, it hurts to think the line ends with me. At least you have Maude and Georgie."

She frowned and wrinkled her brow as if in serious thought. "We need more kids—the bank needs more kids. I can't see myself raising a family at my age."

They shared a laugh. They had already talked for two hours, and Greg had to get back to the hotel and pack his bags. He was going back to Cliff House that evening. Stella and the kids would be there when he got back. He smiled at such a domestic scene.

Penny promised to come to Cliff House for a visit with Harry sometime in the summer—she hated the hot Washington summers. She held him close and kissed him. "Oh, how do you feel about Alice?"

"Alice?"

"Alice Roosevelt."

"I admire her even more than her father."

"Good thinking. Harry and I are attending a small dinner with her."

Gregory left and took a taxi back to the hotel. He thought of Penny and hoped she really was happy. She seemed lonely with Harry away—using half a dozen wartime causes as time fillers. He packed quickly and got to the airport just in time for his flight. His flight went smoothly. Stella was waiting for him at the airport.

When they arrived at Cliff House, Stella said, "Greg, listen. I've just been notified that Buckley is reported missing in action."

"Missing? How did you hear?"

"Yesterday a cable was sent to the bank. Since you were away, I accepted it. There's very little information yet, Gregory." She shook her head. "Buck was on some kind of an air mission. The plane vanished near Tuttlingen, a heavily wooded and dangerous mountain area."

The summer weather in San Francisco produced its ritual morning mists—some called them fog—which would burn off by noon. The port was busier than ever, even though the Germans had given in. The Japanese were being pushed back island by island, and San Francisco was the main port of call for shipping and supplies.

Gregory had taken to frequently writing in his journal. It seemed to have a calming effect on him—especially since Buckley had been reported missing in action.

*　　*　　*

. . . Today, August 6th, a B-29 named Enola Gay dropped an atom bomb on the Japanese city of Hiroshima. It's been estimated a hundred thousand people, mostly civilians, are dead or will die. To write more is to repeat all the banal remarks on the foolishness and cruelty of man to his own kind.

To record two more items. Stella and I are adopting a seven-year-old boy named Bob. His mother and father were killed last month in a small private plane. The mother was a cousin of Stella's, and she's all the family there is.

Stella and I will be married next week, a simple ceremony in the chambers of a judge who is a friend of mine. Marriage was not part of a deal in the adoption of Bob, but it helped make up Stella's mind. Penny said I should bring new Fiores into the firm—so I'm acting on it.

I would be very happy, but Buckley is still listed as missing in action. Jerry Hightower, who has connections inside the War Department, wrote me there are two possibilities (besides the one that Buck is dead). One is that his plane has never officially been reported, or it has been reported as shot down. The whole thing remains a mystery, so he may be lying badly injured in some remote place or be tied up in red tape somewhere in Europe. Or, maybe he's being held prisoner in Russia.

Very weak threads, I admit, but all we have. I remember what my Uncle Fred told me when I was a young soldier: "We are all one fabric with lunatics and criminals . . ."

Book Four

DOUBT

Chapter Sixteen

It was 1946, the year Gregory took Stella to the opening of
Annie Get Your Gun. Georgie went east with Chauncey on their
summer break to see St. Louis win the World Series, and they
sang "Doin' What Comes Natur'lly" at '21.' Laval had been
shot, and Pétain condemned to death. But as Henri Satie said
to his son Paul Achille, "Generals don't shoot generals. The
old bastard will spend some easy time in a clean warm place."

Buckley Fiore, missing in action for a year and a half, got to
Paris the day *Le Monde* printed that de Gaulle had no comment to make on Joe Louis's victory in the prize ring. Buckley had had a hard time of it—first in a Soviet prison camp,
and then in a Chinese prison at Shenyang, all because his
plane got into a crash on a mission to brief some field com-
manders during that rapid advance against the Germans in the
spring of 1945. The plane had run into a storm, been driven
off course, smashed up among Russian-Asian troops. The
pilot died. The soldiers were short, stocky, slant-eyed men of
a far eastern Siberian brigade. Buckley had papers on him,

texts of some general orders, even an item stating that Russia would most likely enter the war against Japan.

The Russians never reported the plane crash. They were sure they had captured a spy. He was in the wrong place with the wrong documents. Now that the war was over, Buckley was free to do as he pleased. His discharge came with a letter from the proper high source, commending him for his "bravery and duty in Java done under harsh and dangerous conditions," and he got a medal.

Gregory spoke to Buckley by telephone. "Maybe you'd like to take it easy in the States. Do a bit of banking here at our San Francisco branch. What you say, Buck?"

"I'd rather go to Paris and help out with the branch there, if it's okay with you."

"Sure, but I do miss you. Henri Satie has got it under control. You need a little thawing out, have some fun."

"Thanks, Greg. And I'll try to figure this Anita La Fiore out once and for all."

"Jesus, she's sent me hordes of letters—actually demanding money from me, but I've been all tied up with bank matters. She seems to be jumping in with both feet, trying to grab a lot of everything to which she might not be entitled. But that's the way the cookie crumbles, doesn't it? Oh, in Paris, you'll find traveler's funds on which you can draw." A pause. "You haven't—fallen in love with her, have you?"

Buckley laughed and scratched his head. "No. Who put that into your head—Joe Dalgaard?" They talked for a while longer—Gregory listening anxiously to Buckley's war stories and remembering how relieved he himself had felt when discharged after two grueling years at war. And he remembered how desperate he was for female companionship. Gregory then realized how worried he was about this girl who claimed to be Buck's half-sister.

*   *   *

Buckley arrived in Paris and went directly to Henri Satie's apartment. Together they went to the Pacific-Harvesters branch. Buckley found the Paris branch to be ample without being oversized, the decor neat and modern, not too ornate. Henri showed Buck to his corner office—already decorated tastefully. Henri Satie introduced Gregory to his son, Paul Achille.

Paul Achille was tall, dark and in his mid-twenties, a handsome nose somewhat bent to one side, dark hazel eyes with long, romantic eyelashes. He was dressed a little foppishly, but that seemed to be the trend, as Buckley observed.

"Papa insists you need help in settling in. But I hear you are an old Parisian." Paul Achille's English was nearly perfect.

"I try. May I stand you a drink at the Ritz bar?"

Buckley looked amused. "A good cognac sounds perfect right now."

Paul Achille Satie was a thoughtful young man but not as intelligent as his father. Over cognac and hor d'oeuvres, they talked about the bank and Paris. Achille said he had been with the French Resistance, assisting the British parachutists at Arnhem. After that he began working for his father at Pacific-Harvesters—a good, stable job in international investments.

"You can do a lot for the firm, Buckley." Paul Achille proved to be a helpful friend to Buckley. He had a respect for money and his job, and yet led an active social life in the nightclubs. He knew many important political and banking people and enjoyed introducing them all to Buckley. Paul even found Buckley a flat on the rue de l'Arcade and helped him pick out the most fashionable furniture. Henri came over with a large bottle of champagne and approved.

"Yes," said Henri. "Comfort with no vine leaves in the hair. Let us give a toast—*l'avenir*."

"Damn close to everything for a jolly good time," added Paul Achille. "Oh, Papa has asked me, Buck, to hunt about in that vague La Fiore business."

"She still in Paris?"

"Doesn't appear to be. But I've the address of her last agent, Jean Tristan Dupin, who handles third-rate opera touring groups in the Middle East and South America."

After father and son had left, Buckley sat by the open French doors of his little balcony. The flat smelled to him of Balzac and Daumier. It felt good to settle down in one spot—free to go where he pleased.

Anita La Fiore, he thought. Gregory had forwarded two letters—not from her, but from a Mexican law firm.

Mr. Gregory Fiore
Director, Pacific-Harvesters Bank

Miss Anita La Fiore has requested us to look into the estate of the deceased Frederick Fiore. Miss La Fiore informs us she will prove her claim if some person of your establishment will contact her through us. Costly legal action can be avoided if we agree to meet on this matter.

The letter was postmarked two weeks ago, and Gregory had noted on it in pencil: "Buck, we will delay until you follow through and advise us."

Buckley took a taxi to the agent Dupin's apartment, a narrow gray building awkwardly pressed between two taller structures. On the door hung a split board lettered J. T. DUPIN, AU PREMIER.

Tristan Dupin was a stocky middle-aged man with tinted brown hair combed forward to hide the spots where it was thinning. On the walls hung a mixed collection of old posters of opera stars from the twenties and photographs of contemporary film personalities.

"Yes, yes, I know Anita. A very talented girl, indeed—maybe a great future opera star."

"Well, you see, she claims to be my half-sister from one of my father's love affairs—with a great singer, Inez Cortez."

"Why yes, Inez Cortez. Anita looks a little like her, you know."

"I know. I really do need to find her. Can you help me?"

"Ah." The man seemed to deflate, smiling sadly. "How do I know if you have good intentions?"

"No, no. There may be something of interest for her. I mean, some kind of settlement to her benefit, perhaps. I can't go beyond that. Can you tell me if she is in Paris?"

He scrounged around in a desk drawer, tossed papers about, inspected an empty ink bottle, threw it into a basket. "She owes me sixteen hundred francs I lended her."

"I'll pay that debt," said Buckley, and handed Dupin a fistful of francs. "Where is she now?"

Tristan Dupin ran a dry hand over his damp forehead. "I am a soft man, you understand; it is because opera is my life. I represent film actors, singers and musicians. But Anita, she used me and then ran away. She is so ungrateful."

Buckley said calmly, "She lived with you?"

The agent sniffed and adjusted his hair. "Oh, yes—she needed a place to stay, and I had a warm bed and a sympathetic ear. Yes, I loved her. There was something different about her. But, but why am I talking to you? It means nothing to you. It was probably just a passing fever."

Clearly the man had been hurt by Anita. He scrawled an address on a piece of paper and handed it to Buckley. Four Casconita Drive, Mexico City.

Buckley thanked Dupin and left him alone with his worries. Buckley wondered if she had gone there to retrieve the documents, or if she was just running away to the only other country she knew. Or was she going to discuss strategy with her half-baked lawyers?

Chapter Seventeen

Buckley found Mexico City a shambles of run-down shacks and dirt. The odor of burned-out wood and the acid smell of wet plaster made him wince. Many roads were blocked, and he saw the remains of blood-red brick walls being pulled down by crews of indifferent workers. It was sad, Buckley thought, to feel no victory here for the population, a mixture of people in worn-out clothes and dirty, barefooted children playing ball in the alleyways. After walking for what seemed like hours, Buckley found Casconita Drive. He walked on until he found small shack with the number '4' painted on the door. He knocked on the door and heard a man shout, "Come in, it's open!"

He opened the door and, to his surprise, found a clean-cut young man sitting at his desk with a stack of papers in front of him.

"Who are you?"

"My name is Buckley Fiore. I'm looking for Anita."

"Mr. Fiore, you can only communicate with our client

through us." He cleared his throat and coughed into his hand. "Unlike perhaps American methods, ours is the proper procedure."

"I understand legal methods, but all I want, first of all, is to talk to Miss La Fiore just as a friend."

"I fear, Mr. Fiore, it is outside the boundaries of how matters are set up."

"What legal claims has she made through you?"

"What is called for, to begin with, is a meeting here, with Anita present, and we can negotiate."

"Have you seen any real evidence? Birth certificate, other documents?"

The lawyer lifted his hands at this preposterous suggestion. "Really, Mr. Fiore, not at all proper."

Buckley said calmly, "I'll be back tomorrow—I need to find a place to stay overnight since it looks like I may be here for a while."

"Good day, Mr. Fiore."

He left, feeling grim. He found a room nearby. Gregory had taught him to expect the world to act for its own best interest and that greed was one part of human nature— Anita's lawyers saw a nice flat fee in the case. Somehow, he still did not believe Anita's story and he certainly didn't trust her lawyer. He would have to find Anita on his own. He walked back to his little rented room and placed a phone call to Gregory, who gave him the phone number of Nat Rosegold, the Fiores' old doctor who moved to Mexico to retire.

As soon as he hung up with Greg, he dialed the number Gregory had given to him. "Hello, Nat?"

"Yes."

"Buckley Fiore, here."

"Jesus Christ, Bucky, how the hell are you?"

"I'm here in Mexico looking up a woman who claims to be Fred's daughter from Inez Cortez."

"Where are you staying, Buck?"

"I've rented a small room about ten miles from where you live, Nat. It's a family matter I'm dealing with, a hassle too mixed up to explain. And I'm stuck in the middle of it, it seems."

"There's more to your story. Tell ol' Doc . . ."

"There's no proof she is who she claims to be." Buckley went into the whole story with Nat Rosegold, who offered to help in any way he could and invited Buckley to come visit at his hacienda and go sailing with him once everything blew over.

"I'll let you know if I need any help, Doc."

"Good luck, Buckley," Nat said before he hung up the phone.

Buckley decided to have dinner at a local bar. An elderly barmaid, thin and nearsighted, set a glass of wine in front of him, leaned on her elbows and stared into space.

"Going to rain?"

"Always goin' to rain." She wasn't the chatty type.

"Theater people, musicians, live around here?"

"Some artistic types and whores."

He sipped his drink and watched a short man at the end of the bar doing a crossword puzzle with a stub of pencil. A clock ticked loudly on the wall. Rain began to splatter the windows, and soon Buckley heard the rushing sound of water spouting from a drainpipe. Somehow he always felt comforted by the rain when he was inside and dry.

Two young men carrying musical instruments came rushing in and proceeded to beat rain from their hats.

"Two gins, Nellie darlin'," said one of them.

121

"Thought you was goin' on tour, boys."

"No, trouble with the bloody unions."

Buckley asked, "You gentlemen with an opera company?"

"Opera?" said the one with the tuba case. "You must be kidding."

"Do you know of any small opera companies hereabouts?"

"Well, now, why you ask?"

Buckley motioned to the barmaid. "I'm looking for a woman who calls herself Anita La Fiore. She is in her early twenties—dark hair and eyes. She sings."

They saluted him with raised glasses, sipped their gin. The tuba player said, "There's a small opera group near here— they perform in the back of a little music shop every other night. I think I remember hearing her name before."

They gave Buckley directions. He paid the barmaid and started walking. The music shop was one small room with a shelf of sheet music. A girl with a pencil stuck in her hair said they were not rehearsing that afternoon. But some of the group "might be back there hackin' about."

"Back there" was a large low room with benches and a platform for a stage. A man in an overcoat and muffler was sweeping up. When asked for Anita La Fiore, he pointed his broom to the right.

There was a strong odor of greasepaint, forgotten remains of sandwiches, and dust. Through an open door he saw Anita in a dressing room with several mirrors, costume racks and battered suitcases. She was bent over a small table eating a flour tortilla covered in brown gravy. When she saw Buckley, she just stared at him.

"Aw, God," she said. She didn't seem too surprised to see him there. She was wearing a puffy red skirt and a blouse which came down over her shoulder.

"So you found me," she said with disdain. "I thought you would have died in the war."

The scene wasn't being played out the way he had imagined it. She rubbed her mouth with the back of a hand and gave a sudden laugh.

"Jesus Christ, you surprised me, Major Buckley."

"I hope so. I've had a hell of a time with your damn lawyer."

"Without those shitty shysters, I might not get what's coming to me, brother." Suddenly she broke out in tears. "It's so hard here, so mean, Buckley. No one, no one to help, to offer a bit of human feeling. Oh, Buckey, I'm so glad you're alive."

He said that he, too, was glad to see her alive.

They talked a lot but didn't touch the subject of her claims to the Fiore family or the documents.

She was living with two girls in the opera company "on two shoestrings and hope." They were looking for backing. The girls lived in a tiny apartment on top of the music store. Buckley suspected would-be suitors were exploited for meals. She looked very thin, her thick loose head of black hair falling down over her shoulders. Her features looked more defined than he remembered.

"I haven't had any good food since you came to see me in Paris two years ago." She sat back contented, a glazed look of satisfaction on her face.

"Save your appetite, Anita," Buck said, "until I have a chance to see those documents." He turned to leave, but then reached in his pocket and pulled out a few pesos and placed them in her hand. "I'll be seeing you soon, Anita."

Chapter Eighteen

Some people said Gregory Fiore devoted himself to Pacific-Harvesters from a rigid sense of duty, something he owed to the family holdings and to Old George. Others said Gregory loved banking, enjoyed the sound and color of the financial world and its challenges.

"Even as a small boy," he explained to Joe Dalgaard at one of their Bay Club lunch meetings, "I'd be taken to the bank and Old George would explain it all to me. Some of it stuck, and some I had to learn all over again."

Yes, the power of the bank and all its branches was impressive—even awesome. It was executor for many of the family estates, and one of the most profitable investments for Pacific-Harvesters was real estate. As the muckraking journalists had pointed out in the past, every sale, every investment for an estate, made rich commissions for the bank. But Gregory was careful to keep an eye on the eager beavers in the bank who handled them. "All we want is our legal pound of flesh."

"Yes, of course, Mr. Fiore, within the penny."

Gregory always arrived at his office early, when the char-women and their cleaning machines were still buzzing about. He'd listen to the hum of the Teletypes, the click of reports of world events being recorded on long ribbons of paper. It was all part of the pulse, he thought, of money activities in Rio, London and Hong Kong.

The bank to Gregory was a symbol of George Fiore's foun-dation—loans to small vineyards, fishermen and bean farmers in the days when the "Anglo banks" ignored them. Now bank clients borrowed on more valuable commodities: wheat, rye and corn. But the bank did most of its business in real estate. Huge buildings were being built along the West Coast now that the war was finally over. Often Gregory dreamed that he had foreclosed on all those new, empty towers, and the structures, animated like Disney characters turned in-sane, were advancing on him in a cockeyed army march, demanding money to feed on, loans and more loans to keep steel-and-glass highrises alive. Then he'd wake to find he had been sweating, and he'd lie very still, trying not to wake Stella.

Gregory felt nervous about all the wartime loans, all the money that had been used to erect shipyards, airplane facto-ries, steel-mill annexes, two big textile mills in Australia for military cloth . . . But now there were those great plants, those empty buildings and all the unemployed workers. It was all beginning to wear him down. He was feeling very old and tired.

Eating his swordfish with Joe at the Bay Club, he noticed the ironic grin on the lawyer's face. "You can grin, you bas-tard, you're not a Fiore, Joe. I'm not happy about today's mergers. The holding companies are taking over all the small businesses, and the sharpies are manipulating stocks of phan-tom corporations."

"Listen, what the Rockefellers and Vanderbilts produced was a series of heirs. That's where you should worry. You need sons and daughters breeding more sons and daughters. Building a team for the future. That's what you need, Greg."

Gregory set down his knife and fork. "Georgie and Maude—both are dating now and may get married soon. Buck, he's very smart. But I don't know if he'll ever marry. He's already getting up there in years. Hell, Joe. I'll hold on as long as I have to."

The lawyer wiped his lips, pointed his napkin at Gregory. "Old George and his brother Fred certainly held up the family erections to create legends. What about little Bob? Show him the ropes now—you'll be surprised how much he'll remember ten years from now."

After his lunch with Joe, Gregory worried that there weren't enough Fiores waiting backstage. But the afternoon was a busy one, and he soon forgot about his worries.

Near three o'clock he decided to make a rare appearance in the offices dealing in commodities. In the great basement he touched the huge circles of the massive standing vaults where security men stood by while trays on wheels were moved in and out. Greg marveled at the huge dials and two-foot-thick doors with all the gears and levers. They were antiques from the early 1900s and would be replaced soon by less cumbersome, more scientific safeguards. In the records department, ranks of adding machines clicked, and entries were made by chattering ribbon-fed numbers. But all this could be out of date soon. He had heard talk at the bankers' convention of something called computers, and the wonder of transistors and robots.

In the counting area coins came spewing out in ordered rolls while whirling machines packed hundred-dollar bills into units and banded them. Gregory read the day's final figures on market advances and losses. Mortgage bonds had to be watched. He set up a deal in which Pacific-Harvesters and Stateside Insurance Company would share in the development of building a sports stadium in Texas. As for the Fiore Vineyard and Napa Jewel Winery, they were showing little profit for the next quarter.

Chapter Nineteen

Buckley was beginning to get impatient with Anita and her lawyer, who had been offering no help whatsoever in the matter of producing any proof of identification that would give Buckley confirmation that Anita was really a Fiore. And Gregory was beginning to put pressure on.

"Let's face it, Anita, I've got to report back on this matter of who you are, and if you are Fred's daughter."

"Oh, my, how serious we are suddenly. Give us a little more time, dear man. Don't spoil a fine day like this."

"Damn it, I must see those documents of yours. You said they were in Mexico. So here I am. Where are they?"

"Buckley, listen to me. I am not Anita La Fiore. I made up the name. My mother was friends with Inez Cortez, and that's how I knew about the story of Inez and your father, Fred. She also told me about Gregory, his nephew—president of Pacific-Harvesters Bank. I was desperate. I had to drop out from the Opera Academy because I could not support myself and pay for school. So I told my agent, Dupin, to give you the address of my lawyer here in Mexico. Who else? He's just a shyster—who else would take on such a case? What did I have to lose? I'm starving and have so much talent to offer." Then she began to cry.

Buckley was stunned. After a little while, he took her head into his hands. He had never known what it was like to live in poverty. But if she was so desperate that she cooked up such a complex scheme, Buckley could not turn away from her now. For the first time, he thought, he could love her without the nagging guilt that she was his sister, and he was relieved. Gregory, too, would be relieved—but *how* could he explain this mess to him? He would have to go back to Cliff House and explain it all in detail. Maybe he would take Anita with him—but then he would be admitting to a very serious commitment with this woman, whom he hardly knew at all. She was a completely different person than she had claimed to be.

She sobbed. "You don't know how hard it is to find people to listen to me, help me with my singing career. Being poor stinks! Without your help, I'll get nowhere. I'll just get older until I'm just crooning in some two-bit café."

He left her littered room and walked silently back to his hotel. It was already dark—he had been with Anita all day.

December 19th, 1946
Lovely downtown Mexico City

Dear Greg:

Here it is nearly Christmas, and I feel I owe you a long, confidential letter as to how I'm holding up, or on to, whatever bit of dignity I have left. I've been over to Paris and have a fine office waiting there. Henri and Paul Achille are doing a bang-up job, and I promised them I'd settle in soon after the New Year. Henri wants to set up banking for some Argentine and Brazilian groups who want to trade coffee and beef for

Italian motorcars, and the Saties, father and son, feel the Latins of South America would favor dealing with an American bank, as their fathers did business with George years ago.

Now, as to the matter of Anita La Fiore. Her story about being Fred's daughter is a lie. I've notified Henri Satie to call off the dogs. She is, just as you suspected, a very poor girl who needs backing for her singing career. Without money, she will get nowhere. Gregory, I really do think we should give her a chance. I think she has great potential—and could even be a very wise investment for us.

Now, as to why this letter is confidential. I have become emotionally involved with this woman. If I tried to explain it all to myself, I'd need a dozen shrinks. I realize Anita herself is not trustworthy. I have become infatuated with a woman whose values are not a shining example of moral rectitude, but then, neither are mine. A woman scheming and seeking to survive, using what methods she can to stay afloat. But, there is something so special about her dedication to becoming a great opera singer.

Reading what I have written, I appear to have contradicted myself a lot—made a patchwork figure of Anita. I've not at all caught her dark stare, her wild moments, her sharp approach to life. She fascinates me, Greg, even her slovenly ways, not caring for dress or neatness, even at times for bathing. So I give up, Greg, trying to explain her to you. I am no critical expert on music, but I think she's quite talented. I tell you, her voice has something no other voice I've ever heard has . . . She needs one big break in the upper reaches of the music world, and I really think I can help her. With this, I will close; I will be in touch with you soon from the Paris branch.

Buck

The letter to Gregory seemed to spell it all out for him, and for the first time Buck was firm in the conviction that he loved Anita. And yet he felt that he could not trust her, and that frightened him. After all, he was a Fiore and he had duties to the family, to Pacific-Harvesters, to a future calm life of a banker with some splendid wife, acceptable to West Coast society. Damn it, she could fit in if she tried. He would buy her some new clothes in Paris and give her money to have her hair washed and combed at a trendy hair salon. With her talent as a singer, she'd soon sweep Parisian society off its feet!

Chapter Twenty

It was a time when Pacific-Harvesters banks were finally set-tling into order—the war was in the past. Banking, Gregory felt, had become a balancing act, and uranium had risen to $1,600 a ton. He wrote financial reports on just how far the bank should support loans to those mines that were riding the atom-age boom. Then there was the matter of the Marshall Plan, twelve billion dollars in European recovery aid. That needed close study and information exchanges with Buckley and the Paris branch. Gregory needed help in making these decisions. Should Pacific-Harvesters extend loans to German industry in support of the Marshall Plan? What if the plan did not aid European recovery? Gregory frequently talked to Buckley over the telephone.

"It worries me, Buck. Pouring out funds over there to cover our enemy's recovery. But if we don't, the Russians will."

"Forget the Russians, Greg, they've got their hands full rebuilding their town that the Germans destroyed. I'm more worried about the Middle East. Now that the Jews have their country back, there's going to be trouble there. Say, did you get my bets on Citation? Great odds! Imagine, Greg, that horse winning the Belmont, the Preakness *and* the Kentucky Derby!"

"Sure I got your bets down, but I didn't bet on Citation myself. Stella favored some nag that came in fifth."

"Everything solid there with Stella and Bobby?"

"Everything's fine, Buckley. How about things with Anita? She become a Parisian yet?"

"Doing fine. Her singing career is really taking off—newspaper headlines and all! Why don't you and Stella come over? We'll show you the champagne town standing on its head."

"Bet you can, but I got to stick around for a while—the damn banking committee is worrying over Latin American debts. Why do we always get stuck down there with what looks very good and ends up with some dictator or general leaving in a hurry with the country's assets and heading for Nice or Monte Carlo?"

"Because we're greedy, or we just love to help people."

"You figure it out. I guess we're all greedy for something."

Buckley sounded okay, Gregory thought as he hung up. If things were shaky with that woman named Anita, it didn't seem to show. Buckley was doing a fine job at the Paris branch and getting along well with Henri Satie. As for Anita, he had read a short item in *Time* magazine:

CENTRAL AMERICA BREEDING GROUND
FOR NEW OPERA STARS?

If a shortage of new Grand Opera stars in the USA and Europe is true, the chili powder and banana countries are hatching a clutch of new voices reaching high pitch, as new talent from Mexico is emerging into the Parisian theaters.

Among the most noted larks is a Venus-shaped soprano,

Anita, who seems to be the cream of the crop. Showered with flowers and praised for a heated Carmen at the Paris Opéra, Anita has been seen on the arm of Buckley Fiore of Pacific-Harvesters' golden nest of San Francisco banking dynasty.

Gregory took Stella and Bobby to the movie *The Bicycle Thief*. When they got home, he rewrote the speech he was to make the next night at the bankers' convention. A Rockefeller would be there, and one of the Rothschilds, and of course, Joe Dalgaard. But mostly present would be well-fed bankers plus a group who were here for a bit of fun, and he'd have to have some of them out to Cliff House. He was to be the host at the convention.

While Greg sat in his library mulling over his speech, Stella and Bobby were playing table tennis, and Bobby was gleefully winning. Bobby, at ten, was growing taller. He was a solid child, not really handsome, but pleasant and likable with a charming smile. He already carried himself like a man, and Gregory already had high hopes for him at the bank. He was a binding tie between Stella and Gregory. They were aware that the boy being in the house made the place come alive, and they were both dedicated to training him properly. They made a conscious effort not to spoil him like Georgie and Maude. Unlike Georgie, Bobby was fascinated by the bank and its intricate operations. He enjoyed being driven to the office by Cody and having lunch with his father and Stella. He could sit for hours next to Stella at her desk, watching her type letters and do calculations. Sometimes he would even greet important bank people who had appointments to see Gregory and proudly show them into Greg's office.

Stella was working only one day a week now, since Bobby was adopted. Marriage had not suited Stella as much as it should have, or so, at times, her husband felt. She had changed in other ways, and Gregory wondered if they hadn't been better adjusted when they were lovers. But Stella was doing a fine job of raising Bobby, and that was very important to Gregory.

And then there were the Fiore parties. Stella was a wonderful hostess. She had adapted to the Fiore lifestyle and never looked back to her past. On Thursday nights they would have bridge parties at Cliff House. Stella was the better player, and they won several cups together—the California Bridge Master Award and the Western Bridge Final. They both played tennis to keep in shape.

Jorgen Dalgaard admired Gregory and Stella, and hoped they would not get stuffy and too settled. All his friends who went to law school with him and pushed their way up and became involved with well-endowed corporations had turned stuffy—talking about tax burdens and servant problems, and their wives worrying about which popular diet to try next, which brand of cosmetics was best for aging skin. Not all people became bores as they aged, thank God, Jorgen Dalgaard thought as he watched Gregory waiting to give his speech at the convention hall. He thought, There are still a few of us, once hell-raisers, going through the motions. Eli Knoles has found the Bath House boys, and Wilma Marx is planting trees in Israel. Seth Smith wrecked a nightclub, Ciro's, down in L.A. There is hope for us old dogs yet.

Waldo Peters of the Great Divide Banking House came up to them at the bar with one of the Rothschilds, and they spoke in French. It was an impressive group of men in the hall. A serious gathering. Wives and mistresses had gone to a showing of the new film *Red Shoes*. Some of the younger bankers had arranged for call girls at the hotel suites. There were introductions and some short organizational items, and then, to a good round of applause, Gregory moved toward the mike, his speech in hand, although he delivered most of it from memory. After the usual platform greetings and a few words from the chairman, some newspaper cameras focused on the speaker. Gregory set down his notes and began to speak in a tone of voice that he hoped was not too cheerful. After all, he was there to discuss very serious issues on banking that Washington was worried about.

"Welcome to San Francisco. I extend a warm welcome from our Bankers' Club. Washington sees our purpose to recommend and suggest action on the problems of the Latin American countries whose debts to American banks are too large and becoming overdue. The war is well behind us now, long enough so that we can pay serious attention to a growing problem that our group will soon present before a Senate Committee. During the last three years, we have been backing Latin American banks in their loans, but now a clearer balance of controls must be put into practice—as outlined by the Assistant Treasury Secretary of International Affairs. This means the banks must be tougher than ever at the bargaining table with Latin American loans. We can now effectively say, 'No money unless you play by our rules and those of the I.M.F.' It also means the banks can take losses on their loans without suffering extraordinary penalties . . ." Gregory glanced at his notes. "We bankers will also be able, as a result of strengthened balance sheets, to consider the Latin American debt problem in a less emotionally charged environment and, we hope, as a series of small separate problems. The bankers can focus on loans to Government agencies . . ."

The rest of his speech flowed easily. When he took his second sip of water, he wondered if Buckley would soon be the one to stand there talking to the big fish and the small fry, to the C.E.O.'s representing Chase Manhattan, Bankers Trust, Morgan Guaranty, First Chicago, First Interstate, Manufacturers Hanover.

He came near to the end of his speech, raised his voice and gave a broad smile. "So now the banks appear to be in their best position in years to be hard-nosed at the bargaining table and to write off loans if necessary without suffering undue financial pain. And that is what I and the group appointed with me will present to the Senate Committee on International Affairs in Washington. Now I think we all need a drink."

There was good, solid applause and even vocal approval. Ducking most of the handshaking, a small group of eight went to dinner at the Blue Fox. The representative from Bankers Trust ordered the best wine in the Blue Fox cellar, and there was brandy later with Chase Manhattan offering a toast: "To Pacific-Harvesters—its standards, its leaders and our host tonight, Gregory Fiore."

He got home very late with the start of a headache, and rather than disturb Stella, he retired to the extra bedroom off his study where he often slept if he came in late. He was feeling he had eaten too much and drunk too much wine and brandy when he fell into a deep sleep.

At breakfast, Stella asked Gregory how his speech went. "It went well. Very well. But I'm tired. Next time, I'm afraid, Buckley will have to represent the bank. I'm just getting too old for this—too many decisions to make and I'm slowing down."

Bobby laughed, and said, "Aw, Dad—you're not old. I'm so proud of you—all the kids at school say their parents just think you're the greatest, really."

Both Stella and Gregory laughed, and Gregory reached his arms over and fluffed the top of Bobby's head, saying, "Well, your mom and I think you're the greatest!"

Cody cleared the dishes from the table, and Stella offered to drive Bobby to school.

Chapter Twenty-one

It was Christmas 1950. Georgie Fiore had been fighting in the Korean War for six months. He had been drafted to the dismay of the entire Fiore family. Penny had tried to get him a letter of deferment through her contacts in Washington, but all attempts at keeping Georgie out of the war were futile.

Sergeant Fiore and three men of his squad, heavily laden with blankets and ponchos over their windbreakers and fur hats with earflaps, sat hunched inside a war-torn tent. Outside the snow fell.

"Jeez," one of the young soldiers said, "you're not afraid, Sarge, that explosive stuff we pulled from that shell isn't going to blow up?" He was wearing a sweater lettered USC under his greatcoat and held a mess tin full of kimchi, rotting fish and cabbage found in a clay pot in the hut. In the cold, the overpowering smell didn't bother them.

"Hell, you're dumb," said another soldier. "It burns clear in the air, explodes only under great pressure."

George Fiore closed his eyes and tried to fight off sleep.

The three soldiers were all that was left of his squad. He wondered if there was any truth to what he had been told by a senior officer—that griping soldiers, as long as they could beef, were still in good fighting shape. He wouldn't bet on the armies retreating down from the north. Big Boy Mac had made his own war, and now he was up his own creek. His United Nations forces were freezing to death. Georgie wondered if anyone at home knew for sure just how bad the disaster was.

A very short, wide black soldier came through an opening in the tent. He was carrying a portable shortwave radio, wore a corporal's stripes and a nonuniform sheepskin jacket. His black face had a blue shine to it, gray in the creases.

"Boy, oh boy, the Korean brass monkeys are sticking to the road." He took a bottle from his pocket and handed it to Georgie. "Try this stuff. None of that local mule piss, this comes from Big Boy Mac's own trailer, which is smashed up in a drift ten miles back."

"Thanks, Shorty." George took a swig and passed it on to PFC Rusloff, who was hunched next to him.

"We still running?"

"Walking in a daze, more like it." Shorty turned on the radio . . . a lot of static, then a voice of a woman singing "C'est si bon."

"Who's in the Rose Bowl?" one of the soldiers asked.

"Who gives a shit?" asked Shorty. "This ain't no Warner Brothers movie. Next you'll be asking me the baseball scores."

Shorty tried to adjust the radio sound. "You guys know who died?"

"Greta Garbo," George said solemnly, taking another swig from the bottle.

"No, Edgar Rice Burroughs."

"Who's he?" asked PFC Rusloff.

"You raised in a cave? Jesus Christ," said Shorty. "You got no education. Just about the greatest writer in the world, that's all. Right, George?"

"If you say so, Shorty."

"I mean, Tarzan, Burroughs done him right—that's why the man's the real McCoy . . . right, George?"

"I'd place him up there with Proust or Joyce." George Fiore was bone-tired, muscle-tired, his stomach was in an uproar. He disliked being a sergeant and being responsible for a squad of soldiers. And most of all, he just wanted the war to end so he could go home, find a girl, maybe get married.

George missed San Francisco and his pals from Yale. He thought to himself that he'd even take a position at his father's bank to get out of this mess.

When he stood up, he felt the pain in his frostbitten toes. "Okay, unless you lugs want to work in a Chinese commie laundry, let's go."

The miserable group packed up the tent and trudged on, following about a quarter mile behind the shuffling massed movement going south. George wondered if Napoleon's retreat from Moscow was as cold, as hungry, as numbing of spirit. Big trucks brought heavy guns in answer to George's thumbs-up. He shrugged and pointed to an escorting car full of officers in heavy wool coats with thick fur collars.

At Kongju the MPs tried to arrest Shorty, claiming the radio was stolen, but he handed over an extra wristwatch and they let him through. Below Chŏnju, the scene got better. There were barracks and a big hospital with real supplies. As usual, Big Boy Mac remained stone-faced as ever in the newsreels in the hospital recovery room. The regrouping was taking place. Tanks just off the ship were being unpacked, as Shorty said, "like Christmas toys." But it was gloomy weather all along the Korean peninsula and in the United Nations' ranks.

The soldiers ate hospital food with relish—Spam, dried eggs and black coffee. Georgie had his frostbitten toes taken care of, and he was running a fever. He went to sleep dreaming about Cliff House. The family was having Christmas Eve dinner. His father sat at the head of the table with Buck and Penny and her husband, Harry. Stella was there, and Bobby was making a fuss because he had eaten too much and had a bellyache. And, oddly enough, Chauncey was there, sharing a private joke and laughing with Maude.

When he woke up from the dream, his big toes had turned black and were peeling off layers of skin like an onion. The nurse assured him that it was a good sign and added that she thought he was really cute. She introduced herself as Shirley. She liked George and managed to stay with him an extra long time on her rounds.

They grew very fond of each other. But then again, George thought to himself, they were both lonely and far from home. "War," George said, "is just not as exciting as it was in the movies." It was not a challenging adventure, but a cold, boring and dangerous step into death. Shirley asked, "Why can't they just settle it like a football game, you think?"

When everbody else was asleep, they smoked Filipino pot together in his bed. After one week was over, George and his three soldiers were ready to continue on their way.

George was involved in a highly deadly frontal attack and lost two more of his squad, leaving only Shorty. He lost weight, and his blood pressure got so low from the attack of fever, he was marked for return to the States.

San Francisco looked splendid and shiny to Georgie from the air, and better when Maude was waiting at the airport to pick him up. He was still a little weak, and Maude had to help him into her car, a tan Mercedes.

She looked very pert, Georgie thought. At twenty-four, she looked like a real woman of the world. Driving away from the airport, she looked at George's shoulders. "You look skinny as a smoked herring, and that uniform was designed for a trained ape!"

"Yes, but you, Maude—damn it—you're all gussied up, a fancy piece."

They laughed and bumped heads, smoked cigarettes and felt warm toward each other.

"How are you doing, my disarming sister?"

"I'm doing pretty well, Georgie."

"Cut the Georgie shit. I'm only two years younger than you. What have you been doing since I left—getting into trouble?"

"I'm working at this local TV station. I'm on for half an hour every morning. It's called, catch this—*From a Woman's Window*. I can do a better news anchor spot than those New York bimbos."

"I'm proud of you—sounds like you're still telling off the world."

"Because right now I'm marking time, interviewing moronic lady authors of shitty bestsellers, mixing salads with secret ingredients. I even do the weather. But, Georgie, I'm just waiting for a big break at CBS or NBC!" She flipped her cigarette out the window and he noticed the blue touched-up eyelids and rouged cheeks.

"I still have another year at Yale. Maybe in a couple of months I can go out on a dig in Jordan. Maybe Yale will recommend me."

"Christ, do you remember digging that mission ruin up at the lodge while Chauncey and I were looking for turtles?"

"Chauncey was drowned, with most of the crew. His Navy supply ship hit a drifting Chinese mine."

She said nothing. They were entering the city, and the morning mist had burned away from silver to yolk yellow. The streets were bustling, and it amazed George how little it had changed and to see the indifference to the horror of lost battles that had consumed so many young men. He wondered if Maude would ever understand what he had seen and been through for the past year. Or would she, like most people in the streets, just pretend that nothing unusual was taking place?

"Your job pay enough for this car?" George asked.

"Not likely. Dad gave it to me last birthday. Tell me, how bad was it out there?"

He smiled and pinched his sister's arm. "It was bad, *real* bad. You kill them, they kill you. You roll in the mud, you freeze in the winter. Everything has a bad stink. You eat it, you drink it, swim in it, breathe it. It's bad beyond bad."

"Even the girls?"

"Aw, come on—is this a TV interview? It's as easy there to get V.D. as postage stamps. In the hospital there was this nurse. I liked her a lot. She was from New York. She kept me from wanting to die."

They were approaching the Pacific-Harvesters building.

"Dad will give you a pep talk about working at the bank."

"Don't worry." He crossed two fingers. "I've resisted his charm so far."

"Charm, my ass," said Maude as they drew up to the curb and the doorman rushed out. "Dad is damn serious. As he sees it, who the devil is going to take over this dynasty?" She laughed. "God, that sounds corny. But Dad is corny . . . but sweet."

"Mornin', Miss Fiore," said the doorman.

"This is my brother, George."

"So it is. Never would have known—thinned out so. Welcome back, sir."

"Happy to be back, Dooley."

They took the elevator up to Gregory's office, and the secretary led them right in. A new air-conditioning unit hissed politely against an outer wall. Maude stood back and fought back a tear. She was so happy her brother was alive.

"I'll leave you two to talk," she said, kissing George and putting an arm around his neck. "I'll set up a big party for you . . . I feel lousy about Chauncey!"

George sat facing his father, not fully at ease. How old he looked, the gray thinning hair, the strong face, handsome but beginning to sag. It was the first time George had ever thought of his father as being an old man. They talked of the war. Gregory smoked his pipe and offered George a Havana cigar.

"We have your old room ready for you at the house. Stella and Cody are expecting you." Gregory cocked his head to one side. "Unless you'd like to set up a flat for yourself."

"No, I'd like to stay with you and Stella. She sent me a few letters. How is she?"

"Oh, Stella is fine; changed a bit, as we all do."

"And Bobby?"

"Oh, he's fine. Getting good grades in school."

"I suppose you want to know what I want to do now that I'm out of the army."

"I certainly would."

"I'd like to finish up at Yale and get my masters in archaeology, and I'm hoping to go out with a dig in Jordan."

Gregory tapped his fingers on the desktop. "Dangerous. The Arabs are planning to massacre all the Jews in Israel."

"I feel I need to give it a try."

145

Gregory stiffened. "Don't be so stubborn. Look, George, bullshit aside, the bank is what the Fiores are. Yes, we make a great deal of money, and sometimes a loss here and there. But to Old George, to my father, and my uncle Fred, it was a challenge. Damn it. Pacific-Harvesters is one of the props that keeps this country rolling. So we have to keep its foundation strong. This chair, this desk, this office, this building, and what goes out of it, is sacred to the Fiore name. That's why, George, I need you and Buck—and someday Bobby." He picked up the pipe and gave a shy grin. "Christ Almighty, listen to me—I made a speech."

"Yes, Dad. But don't bank on me. I really don't care for bank balances. I'm going to Jordan if I can. I won't change my mind, Dad."

They stared at each other for a moment in silence. George sighed, stood up and walked to one of the great windows, looking down on the busy street. He felt badly about disappointing his father, but he knew he had to go out after what he wanted. He only wished it was what his father wanted.

"I'm sorry, George, deeply sorry. I'm going to do something that hurts me greatly. George, I'm going to disinherit you."

George took the cigar from his mouth. "From what?"

Gregory came back to his desk. "You hold in a trust fund that your mother set up for you and Maude, a nice stack of bank shares. The income will give you enough to live comfortably." He went over to his son, who was standing at the window still looking the other way, and put an arm around his shoulder. "I still love you. You are my son, pigheaded as you are. I hope you make something of your life."

George tossed the lit cigar into a large ashtray. "But goddamn it, you are booting me out of the family."

Now Gregory showed his temper. "You said it, George.

You still have a choice. You can make up your mind to take what I'm offering you at the bank. But, if you don't, you walk out that door and don't come back in."

George shook off his father's arm and laughed coolly. When he spoke, he had just a slight twitch. "Okay, Pop, it's been a face-off. We know how we stand. It's just like you said, Dad. I'm walking out the door—don't you doubt it, I'm never coming back."

Before Gregory could protest, he was gone. He had expected screaming, raving, a broken vase, an overturned chair. But this exit had left him dumbstruck.

Book Five

TRUST

Chapter Twenty-two

The Paris branch of Pacific-Harvesters had expanded. When Gregory, Stella, Maude and Bobby came to Paris in the fall, there was a large but discreet sign of gold and black, and an entrance of inoffensive modern decor with a cool and calm interior, well-lit waiting rooms and tastefully decorated offices—"that sense of atmosphere," Henri Satie said, "that could only be indicative of prudent business, good taste and manners, which indicated knowledge about money and international affairs one could trust."

Paul Achille, besides serving Pacific-Harvesters, had his own firm in a tall modern building near the Pont Neuf, Satie International et Cie, which dealt with clients from Lebanon to Singapore in transfers of credit and numbered Swiss bank accounts.

Henri Satie was getting old and slowing down, but still advised Buckley on his dealings with the French government.

Buckley and Anita led an active social life, but their often wild bohemian existence was over. Buckley was graying at the temples, and he left the wilder entertaining of American clients to Paul Achille.

Buckley was very much in love with Anita, although he denied himself the ache of thinking back too often to those days in Mexico. They were a very attractive couple and had thrown some of the most talked-about parties in Paris. Buckley decided to marry her, despite the fact that Gregory had tried to persuade him not to. "She's unpredictable, Buck, not a good example for a banker's wife."

But Buckley reminded him that she was capable of producing a healthy batch of Fiores, and that ended the conversation.

The morning after he proposed to Anita, Buckley went to the most fashionable jeweler in Monte Carlo and bought her a four-carat diamond ring. It was announced a week later at the George V to a small gathering of some of their friends from the bank and from the Paris Opéra. Anita looked very lovely in pale blue with the family emeralds, her face flushed, and she took the well-wishing with grace, having belted away a brandy before the press came in with notebooks and cameras. The Saties hosted the event, and the waiters in the private party room passed around champagne. Maude had a wonderful time—surrounded by young bankers. Stella and Gregory had the first dance.

They decided to hold the wedding the following month. Buckley and Anita began looking for a larger flat near the Sacre Coeur, as well as a little flat in London so they could slip away from Paris whenever they wanted to get away.

"I believe in marriage," said Henri Satie one day over lunch. "It is never perfect, but it has its virtues—it calls for tolerance, understanding and making an effort."

Buckley thanked him for his advice. "As they used to say to the bartender on the Western frontier, 'I'm willing to try anything once.'"

Buckley knew it was time for a change in his life. He was mature enough to handle marriage, and the future would be the bank, a home, children. It was very late, and Buckley was going over some stock reports before Anita came home. Lately she had been rehearsing her role in *Carmen* and wasn't coming in until long after Buckley had fallen asleep.

Chapter Twenty-three

Buckley and Anita inspected a unit in a house in the Île de France with a grand staircase, a spacious courtyard, a coach house for their cars and living quarters for the servants. Back in the bare living room, Anita paced off floor space. "It's just right for the sofas we bought. There's even a room for a den for you, darling."

"I'd rather call it a study, Anita."

"Of course . . . a study."

The agent pointed to a marble fireplace, which was carved with a coat of arms. "Once the Orléans branch. During the revolution, the queen was to be smuggled out of France after being hidden in this house. Someplace here is a hidden passage that hasn't yet been found."

"Good for playing hide-and-seek," Buckley said, looking at his watch and motioning to the agent to get down to facts. He left a deposit in the name of Mr. and Mrs. Buckley Fiore, although the wedding was still a month off. Buckley thought it would be best to be married by the town's mayor in the city hall.

Anita laughed cheerfully. "I know you're joking, darling. I may only have my friends from the opera, but I want a grand wedding and a gorgeous wedding dress. I know it's all stupid, all this swank about ceremonies. But there it is. I want to get married in style."

It was Henri Satie's son Paul Achille who came up with a happy solution, "a proper *lever de rideau*": a simple ceremony at the French embassy by a visiting Anglican bishop. Then a dinner at Maxim's in a private set of rooms.

"Would the embassy agree?" asked Buckley.

"Of course," said Paul Achille. "My father has connections there. His old friend is the American ambassador to France."

Buckley shook his head and laughed. "I hope for Anita's sake they agree."

They signed a long-term lease on their new home, and contractors were brought in to batter down walls, put in pipes, replace old kitchen ranges and historic snorting water closets. Anita took all of this in stride. She could haggle with plumbers, beat down rug dealers and order re-laying of the new oak floor done in the wrong style.

"You're a champion," Buckley told her, walking around a partly torn-down wall and over ladders, bulky crates and lengths of timber and pipes.

Anita, in chic work slacks, hair tied up in a blue band, was full of pride, blueprints under one arm and drinking coffee from a paper cup.

"Well, Buck. How am I doing so far?"

"You're doing fine, Anita, just fine. After the wedding,

we'll take a long honeymoon, and by the time we get back, it will all be finished."

She wrapped her arms seductively around his neck. "Oh, Buckley. Can we go by ship? Maybe to the Greek islands?"

Buckley remembered that Nat Rosegold owned a house boat somewhere in the Greek islands.

Buckley nodded his head. "Greek islands? I'll give old Doc Rosegold a ring and ask him if we can stay at his houseboat. It's right on the beach, and I'm sure he'll let us use it! He lives on an island the tourists have never set foot on. I'll get right on it."

Buckley thought of Doc's houseboat—was it on a lake in Kashmir? He was impressed, a bit awed, by Anita's energy; how excited she was about getting married. He had seen a drastic change in her since he had proposed to her. She was no longer frivolous and wild. Buckley sensed that as a married man his life would be laid out for him like a dress shirt and studs for some fancy dinner. But, after all, he did have to settle down now and raise a family. Just then the phone rang and interrupted his thoughts. It was Greg. He called to tell him he and Stella and Maude would be coming to Paris to attend the wedding.

"And George?"

"I don't know, Buckley. It's a long story. I'll tell you everything when I see you."

The next day Buckley received a letter from George. The wedding invitation had reached him after much handling and stamping by postmasters of the western Himalayas, reaching him at the Lamayurn Monastery in Nepal. George was living in a mud hut. The weather was so cold, even the fire of cow dung and twigs didn't keep it out. George had gotten used to drinking brick tea mixed with rancid butter, millet gruel and tough goat singed but still raw inside. While the whiskey lasted and the weather did not get more than twenty below, he could continue to set up the cameras for photographing the murals of the monastery, as well as whatever had survived of the Tantric manifestation of the Eight Auspicious Symbols.

It was there at Lamayurn that Norman Broadbill, a professor from Yale, had fallen twenty feet off the scaffolding and broken his arm. George could hear Norman moaning two mudrooms down and the drone of the monk with the spinning flywheel's rotating prayers reciting the call to Vishnu Balarama. He put more dried dung on the tiny fire and reread Buckley's wedding invitation.

George made himself comfortable on the air mattress under the sleeping bag, the extra sheepskins. He was there because he had missed the swank dig in Jordan. As he wrote Buckley, "That fancy expedition took only assistants whose parents' estates could endow a dig with special air-conditioned trailers or help to erect a wing at the university named for some fossil digger. Thanks for the invite, Buck. Can't tell if I'll be able to make it, but save a seat for me, will you? But, please, nowhere near my old man—as you know, we're not on speaking terms. Hope to see you soon, George."

There was one other graduate student besides George on the expedition. Isadora Mercer was an intellectual with horn-rimmed glasses who was writing her thesis on primitive art. Her uncle, Harry Mercer, was also on the trip. Uncle Harry had put up the money for Norman Broadbill. He had formerly been involved with the university arts and humanities department. He and Professor Broadbill were under contract with a publisher of art books to bring out a volume of the color photographs. George had been very lucky to be invited on the expedition. The Hungarian cameraman who was to go along with the group had fallen off a bridge and drowned in an icy stream on his way to meet Broadbill at the foot of Nanga

Parbat. Norman Broadbill offered George the position of photographer, telling him to pack up and that they would be leaving in the morning. Norman Broadbill, George figured, was either English or Irish, a sort of gypsy scholar who wandered from university to university and, from time to time, published a popular book. "Other professors, who have envied my sales in the past, condemn me as a popularizer." His recent books had failed to sell. "Today, George, neither publishers nor the American public want serious books by serious scholars. Glad to have you on board."

George was aware this was no vitally important expedition, and its only merit was nothing more than a rich man's whim to be a new art publisher. But it was a dig, and he enjoyed flying to Nepal with Mercer, Broadbill and Isadora. George enjoyed getting back in touch with nature, even the rough weather and coarse food, the smell of acrid smoke from the dung fires. Harry Mercer had brought along two cases of Dewar's Scotch and sour mash bourbon. Isadora fit right in with the group. She was self-sufficient and strong enough to handle herself well with no luxuries—maybe even better than George.

Isadora was somewhat of a problem to George. She was aggressive and not very feminine. She was very well-rounded and seemed to know something about everything. In a way, she intimidated George, who often felt ignorant around her. She was engaged to a poet whom she planned to marry when the expedition returned to New York, but it was good to have a young man on this wild trip. Sometimes, before turning in at night, she read some of her fiancé's shorter poems to George, and when he made no comment, she said, "Pretty deep, huh?"

And he would reply, "Sure, real deep."

But his reaction to the poetry was so casual, she stopped reciting it for him. George took photographs of flaking rose and green walls with the big camera Gregory had bought for him before he went to Yale. He had them developed in Nepal before plunging further into the wild mountains.

Both Harry and Norman said they were just what they had wanted. "You're a good man, George." They were glad to have George along.

George realized they knew nothing about good photography, but he was enjoying himself, and so the group moved from the Taleju Bhavani temple to the Thirse Monastery on the Panchhavaktra, Norman marking their way on his maps.

One night Isadora, who had stopped talking of her poet, moved closer to George. "Can I borrow some of your warmth?"

"Whatever I can spare." She snuggled into his sleeping bag and George quickly turned the other way. He did not want to get involved in something he'd be sorry about later. George took Buckley's note out of his pants pocket and bumped Isadora.

"I'm only staying one more week. We're almost out of film, and a relative is getting married in Paris. I want to be there."

"Fuck you, too," said Isadora. "You and I had great possibilities, George. Now things are becoming uncomfortable and the weather's getting more bitter and you decide it's time to go."

The next few days were awkward between Isadora and George. A guide had been sent up to take George to a small airport. He promised Norman and Harry he would have all his rolls of film developed as soon as he got to Paris and send them in care of the Yale department of archaeology.

He parted from his guide at a dangerous-looking airport. The rickety plane ran into a storm. George had hidden a flask of Jack Daniels and shared it with a fat Hindu sitting next to him. The storm had passed, but they ran low on gas, landing somewhere in Kathmandu.

Chapter Twenty-four

The gathering of the Fiores in Paris for the wedding included representatives from *The New York Times* and *The New Yorker*.

There was no public notice of George Fiore's arrival from India. He looked lean and weather-beaten. Gregory greeted his son with admiration.

"You really enjoyed all that mountain climbing?"

"Roughing it really isn't so bad, Dad. Good for the spirit. How good you look, Stella." He hugged his stepmother and kissed her cheek. He actually did not think she looked her best. Stella had aged more than he expected; but then he still remembered her when he was much younger and they had frolicked together at the lodge.

"Where's Maude?" he asked.

"She'll be coming," said Buckley, feeling overdressed in morning coat and gray-striped trousers. "She's in London covering some government upset for CBS."

"Imagine our Maude consorting with the big fish in England."

Everyone thought Anita looked splendid but a bit stiff in a French creation that was considered high-fashion chic. Buckley thought she looked radiant and looked forward to being alone with her.

Henri and Paul Achille arrived at Maxim's with some rare bottles of wine, as well as those friends of Buckley's who had known him as Major Fiore in the war. It soon developed into a very warm, cheerful reception. Some guests were dancing and singing while some others had a spirited debate about the younger generation with their noisy music and how the cost of everything had gone up.

Buckley managed to get George into a room off the party area where they could sit and talk without being disturbed.

"You really intend to go on with this expedition beat, I mean, as a career?"

"Oh, hell, Buck, I get questions like that from Dad, not you. So far, it's what I like to do. I mean the rough outdoor life, going to places where I've never been. And, maybe, someday I can contribute something very unique to society, which is more than I can say for being a damn banker."

"George, I think you're just scared that you won't be able to live up to your father's standards."

"Look, Buck, don't try to psychoanalyze me. I know what I want, and I don't want to work at the bank—at least not now."

Buckley refilled George's glass of champagne. George sipped. "You're planning to give me the bank pitch, aren't you, Buck?"

"Why the hell not? Pacific-Harvesters needs you more than some cockeyed wilderness with no road signs. You're the right age, you're finished with college. Bobby has the interest but he's much too young. Gregory insists he go to college first."

"Well, Buck," George said, grinning and leaning his head against Buckley's shoulder, "you're married now and can breed and breed, you and Anita. I can tell she can produce litters of Fiores. So many you'll have to open more banks to get them all working for good old P-H."

"You've had too much champagne."

"It's good to drink fine champagne after the native brew of millet and bird droppings. I'm sorry. I guess I'm a little looped. All I can say is I'll think about it, Buckley." Then he stood up and said, "Time to go, Buck. Your guests are waiting." George put his arm around his cousin's shoulders and they walked together in silence to the party room.

Anita ran to the door and grabbed Buckley by the arm. All of her was there and real, tugging at one of his arms. "Come, darling, the photographer is here from the Paris *Herald-Tribune* to take our picture."

It was a picture that would be reproduced in most of the New York and San Francisco newspapers, and was the first item Anita pasted into the embossed blue and gold leather album bought at Les Galeries Lafayette.

That evening Gregory and Stella prepared for bed in their hotel suite in the slow ritual of undressing that they had grown accustomed to.

"Buckley's looking very happy, don't you think?" asked Stella, rubbing scented cream into her face and neck.

"You think so?" He turned to study his wife's face.

"Yes, I do."

Gregory was in a dressing gown after brushing his teeth and examining his gums with a grimace in the mirror. "Frankly, I thought he looked a little scared."

"Why should he be, Greg? She's a lively, wonderful girl and she adores him. In a very romantic way, of course. I think she is good for Buckley. She's exciting, warm and he'll never get bored with her."

"Damn it, Stella, you know very well that she is wild—she is very different from us."

Gregory went to open a window partway; the late rumble of night traffic came up, and a light breeze stirred the drapes. He felt it would be foolish to carry the conversation further.

Maude came over from London to visit George. She was wearing a mannish hat with a raffishly cut suit of dark wool. In one arm she carried two shopping bags, and in the other a portable typewriter. George met her at Orly. After they hugged and kissed, Maude stepped back to examine her brother.

"God, Georgie, you look like Gary Cooper with a sunburnt nose."

"Mountain windburn. And you look like Dotty Thompson playing Robert Taylor in drag."

"Easy there, boy, you're talking to a powerful maven in the news media. How's the bridegroom?"

"Bewildered, I think, but the bride is a pip. Very mysterious, I think, but a good sport."

"And Mom and Dad?"

"Like kids on holiday in Paris, but in slow motion."

In the taxi back to Paris, they talked of themselves, of their childhood, of Maude's reporting career at CBS—she dropped names with a natural ease. George expanded on the wild frontiers beyond India—the expedition and Isadora. They were very happy to see each other. The two of them were so close and yet, Maude thought, friendly rivals. They always competed for who had the more exciting story to tell.

Maude had made great progress as a television reporter and host. She had a weekly radio broadcast to America from Europe, and she was currently working on a documentary film idea she had presented of touring European cities to see how they had recovered from the war.

"Television has got to go beyond game shows and *Lucy*. It seems that everybody is compulsively glued to the box every night, like a disease. I want them to be watching me—the big broad on the airways. Georgie, what about you?"

"First, it's George, not Georgie. And I have no plans of being a big star. I want to travel everywhere and go on some real archaeological digs, even get into Tibet. That would make Dad's eyeballs pop."

"Any plans for marriage?" Maude winked slyly at her brother.

"Not for a long time, Maude. And you?"

Maude laughed and said, "I prefer 'rocking around.' More freedom and variety."

All the Fiores were having a wonderful time in Paris. Buckley and Anita were getting ready to go on their honeymoon to the Greek islands. It turned out that Doc Rosegold invited them to stay with him on his houseboat at Aztos. George was on speaking terms with Gregory, and they even spent a day touring the museums together while Stella and Maude shopped in the overpriced fashionable shops—Poche, Vendrenne, Hermès. They all met for lunch in the Eiffel Tower.

Henri Satie invited all the Fiores for dinner at his home, a rare French treat. As Buckley explained, "The French do not let Americans into their personal home life, no matter how close you may be with them in business matters."

The Saties lived in a large flat on the rue Duphot decorated with ornate furniture of various periods, ancient wallpaper and valuable paintings. Stella noticed a Monet and a Turner among them. Madame Satie was plump and making no attempt to hide her gray hair. She presented a grand meal, and Henri Satie announced each course in French with an English translation. The Saties—even the children, Rémy, Céleste, Hilaire, Thérèse and Jacqueline, and of course, Paul Achille—all spoke English in varying degrees of fluency.

"A fine family," said Gregory to Henri and Madame Satie.

"*Ah, oui,*" replied Madame Satie. "Not here with us tonight is our married daughter Camille with her husband in Lyons and twins, Sidonie and Bertrand. They are skiing at Chamonix."

Paul Achille and Maude were not present at the dinner. They were following the professional bicycle racers on a run from Reims to Bourges with Maude's television camera crew. It had been a spur-of-the-moment inspiration, as Paul Achille called it, for him to come along. He and Maude had enjoyed a great week in Paris. Paul took Maude not only to the basilica at the Sacré Coeur and the Jeu de Paume, but also to some of the wild places of entertainment and cabarets in a mingled atmosphere of drink, smoke and unwashed bodies.

Paul Achille, at thirty, had a realistic outlook on his future. He had danced and tasted many sides of life and was now ready to settle down to respectability, maybe even get married and raise a family. Paul Achille had a special attraction to Maude. He was delighted with her company. On the practical side, Maude Fiore was an heiress; her shares in Pacific-Harvesters stock were invaluable. Paul Achille, standing on the balcony of his flat, smoked a cigarette before retiring after a delightful night out with Maude at the Shéhérazade. His mind and his emotions seemed in conflict.

Yes, he could easily fall in love with her. He tossed the cigarette away, watching it fall into the small garden below, making a trail of sparks. He thought to himself, What if she was not Maude Fiore? Yes, he would love her just the same. He thought of telling her he loved her, but he had only known her for one week! He went to bed telling himself he would not make a fool of himself. Take Buckley and that whore of an opera singer. I will not wriggle like a trout on a hook. I will take my time and analyze my situation with her before jumping off the deep end. He did not sleep well that night and awoke early in the morning feeling very groggy.

Alone in his office, Paul Achille busied himself watching what South Africa would do about the release of gold from its mines. Late in the afternoon he would have to go to a long meeting to discuss which stocks to buy and which to sell. He felt detached as he watched the returns. It was as if he were watching figures run their foolish rounds in a silly game. Actually, he was ahead as the morning trading ended. He had a two-thirty appointment with his father and Buckley to talk about a new Swiss setup for which some American hotshot and his salesmen were selling shares to investors.

Henri Satie waved it off. "It can't amount to anything. It's all puffery."

Buckley asked, "But are we going to miss out on something very valuable if we don't bid?"

Henri Satie pursed his lips. "Well, Buck, you never can tell what greed will do to people. Look, Paul just did his annual forecast. We don't have any real money in our bank vaults to match the sums we mark down in depositors' records. Stocks and bonds change hands all the time."

Paul Achille interrupted. "There are hog-belly futures, piggies growing up.

Buckley poured Henri Satie a glass of mineral water. His liver was aging badly. "We'll keep an eye on this Swiss setup for you, Henri."

Henri wiped his lips, pressed a hand on his liver area. "The idea is not new. Will you join us at the opera with the Fiores tonight, Paul?"

"Sorry, Papa, I'm going with Maude to the Palais des Sports. She has a CBS television crew making a documentary there."

Buckley grinned. "Watch yourself, Paul—Maude is a balls breaker."

Paul Achille had little interest in the backstage life at the Palais, the odor of rubbing liniment and sweat. Maude seemed to function well in this world of great arc lights and black cables. The cameras focused on her from time to time as she explained what the oafs were doing with their muscles, while somewhere a band played circus music that gave Paul a headache.

That night he asked Maude to go to bed with him. They were in his Mercedes driving through the streets of Paris. It was well after midnight, and Maude was exhausted. Men with hoses were washing down sidewalks, and water wagons were parked in the alleys. They drove on in silence, and Maude did not reply until Paul parked the car in front of his flat.

"I am not going up to bed with you."

"But it would seem—"

"Listen, Paul, this is not going to be any one-night stand!"

"Maude, I care for you, and it seems it's the natural thing to do."

"I have a career, you have a career. I can't be involved in any love affair. I just don't have the time or the energy for it. Paul, I like you a lot, but love. No, *mon cher*."

They sat silently in the dark car. Paul wished it was all only a movie. He would casually take out his cigarette case and

offer her one, and they would light up and talk romantically
about nonsense. Instead, he just took her hand and earnestly
tried to say the right thing.

"Our worlds touch. There isn't any reason for us to play
games. I didn't plan to fall in love, *faire l'amant*."

"Jesus, Paul, I know, I know. How do you think I feel?
I've got to give all my energy to that goddamn camera crew
and director. I've a career which I have to devote my ambi-
tions to. God, Paul, I'll admit I've never felt about any man
the way I feel for you. I don't enjoy it. In fact, I'm scared of
these feelings."

"I know. I don't like it either. But it's only our first reaction. He suddenly asked, "You ever read Stendhal's *On
Love*?"

She groaned and lifted her hand as if to protect herself.
"Please, no textbooks. Yes, I've read his ideas; love is a twig
in a wet saltmine and it becomes covered with crystals of salt.
Love can crystallize around you whether you like it or not."

"I never knew you were so bright, Maude." Paul laughed
and helped her out as she slid over. "This, Miss Fiore, is a
strange hour, a not particularly pleasant spot with the
trashcans at the curb. But—"

"My God. You're going to propose to me!"

"Clever girl." He put his arms around her, they kissed and
then she pushed him away. "Drive me to my hotel and cool
off. Tomorrow I have to go out again early for the bike race
down south. Let it rest, Paul. Think it over until I get back."

"Nonsense. I'll come along. I was planning to go south
anyway—to look at a coin collection which my old uncle has
wanted to show me. He's a priest on the Côte d'Azur at
Menton. So, you see, I'm going too."

"You're a persistent bastard, Paul."

"Now you know me."

He drove her to her hotel, with one hand on the wheel and the other holding Maude's. They didn't speak, just stared straight ahead. Maude thought to herself, All that fancy language that serves poets sounds false and pretentious at a time like this. So, in silence, they kissed again when they reached her hotel, and the only thing she said before getting out of the car was, "We start at ten in the morning from the Lutétia-Concorde, in three buses. Good night!"

"*Ma chère*," Paul said. As he left her, he wondered what his father would say in the morning when, as a dutiful son, he made his announcement.

Chapter Twenty-five

Buckley and Anita's son was born in 1960 on the same day the Soviets shot down an American U-2 spy plane. After much deliberation about his name, Buckley and Anita finally agreed on George Andrew. Maude and Paul Achille showed up for the baptism.

Maude, as godmother, held George Andrew. Anita glanced at her husband, who was grinning proudly from ear to ear, while the priest touched George Andrew's brow and lips with a dot of oil.

"Benedicat vos omnipotens Deus . . ."

The baby yawned and gave a small cry. His nanny, Miss Drucilla, who would take over, took a step forward but retreated back to her seat as Anita shook her head. Father Ruskin smiled, and Maude handed George Andrew to his mother. Paul Achille and Henri Satie shook Buckley's hand, and kissed Anita. *"En vérité,* a fine event."

Maude said to Anita, "Wonderful ceremony, and George Andrew played his part like an actor at the Old Vic. Now, darlings, I must be off, this damn U.S. spy plane matter, the U-2 shot down over Russia. I'm interviewing the Soviet chargé d' affaires in twenty minutes for overseas television."

Maude and Paul had been married for two years and already had twins, Gigi and Georges. *Time* magazine had reported:

> Few can imagine that the fiery CBS news maven and star journalist is the mother of twins—one-year-old Gigi and Georges. To her bow bankers, diplomats, film stars, fashion kings. She is honored and respected. Spending an hour with Maude Fiore means facing her deep, probing interviews that dart like a rapier. Her NBC rival, Snow Williams, merely shrugs her off. "She is too noisy and very condescending to those beneath her, too kiss-assy to those above her."

Actually, Maude that year had done her most talked-about interviews before and after the Kennedy-Nixon debates. She would also soon beat the news services on the fact of Adolf Eichmann's arrest by the Israelis on a tip from Doc Rosegold, who had connections inside Israel.

Little Bob had grown up quickly and was finishing up his last semester at Harvard. Gregory and Stella did not come to Paris for the christening of George Andrew; Gregory's back had been bothering him lately. His back was x-rayed by the family doctor who diagnosed a displaced disk in the spine. He was instructed to stay in bed for two weeks and take muscle-relaxing soma pills.

"Can I use the goddamn telephone?"

Stella moved the phone to Gregory's night table. "You can call the Pope, the Kremlin and the North Pole for all I care. But don't move from that bed. You should be in the hospital, not here at home. The doctor is sending over an ugly bright nurse."

171

Gregory and Stella did talk to Buckley, and the baby was held to the phone. Anita swore George Andrew made a sound close to "Hi."

Gregory and Joe Dalgaard had tickets for the Sugar Ray Robinson middleweight championship fight, but Gregory was still bed-bound, spending a lot of time doing exercises for his back. After two weeks he was granted three hours a day at the bank.

Cody Hutton was getting old and wasn't much use around the house anymore, but he and Gregory still played cards at night.

George was the only Fiore not alarmed by the U-2 being shot down. He was in a mine layer called the *Enterprise*, moving in the Arctic Lagoon off the island of Sarichef, which consisted mostly of rock and swamp. Nothing much grew but low, wind-tormented shrubs, moss and lichen. Sarichef was marked on the ship's map as just east of the International Date Line. To the west, George could only see the slate-gray sea; some place beyond was Siberia, the area used for air defense by the Soviets.

George beat his gloved hands together and turned on the ship's bridge to Silas Punt. Silas Punt was a Nobel Prize winner for his original work in vitamins and his discovery of a new chain of carbons in certain fossils. He carbon-tested deposits of burned-out wood on Sarichef that might be twenty-five thousand years old.

"We will prove man came across to Alaska on some kind of bridge from Siberia at least twenty-five or thirty thousand years ago. The ancestors of the American Indian!"

"Somebody has, Silas."

"No one, my friend, puts that event back more than fifteen thousand years. A mere yesterday. But twenty-five thousand, eh, George? We'll astonish the world!"

172

George and a crew of natives from Sitka were going to dig for an ancient native village in the marsh and bogs of Sarichef Island to prove Silas Punt's theory.

The icy fog was thicker, and the captain of the *Enterprise* was sounding his foghorn at closer intervals. George went below and decided to write a letter to Maude, saying that if they didn't prove Punt's theory in one month, he would be heading home to San Francisco for a while.

Anita's singing career was reaching its peak. On the posters all around the world where she appeared, the name of LA FIORE was printed larger and larger, and the titles of the operas smaller and smaller. She was the raging soprano. The press coverage of her career moved at times from the musical review columns into the news sections. Her personal life, real or media-invented, was of international news value. Buckley sometimes traveled with Anita when he could get away from the bank while Miss Drucilla stayed at home with George Andrew.

If the musical critics grew somewhat caustic in their reviews of her, they had to admit her Contessa in Mozart's *Le Nozze di Figaro* was the best of her period, and the power in her Marschallin in the *Rosenkavalier* was unrivaled. Her moods were part of her media attraction. She screamed at managers, damaged her dressing rooms and was frequently late to rehearsals. The gossip columnists rumored that her marriage with Buckley would not last and that he was bringing up the child by himself. When asked, Buckley just said he'd settled into fatherhood, into an image of a popular American banker in Paris. At times it rather amazed him. There had been no great strain with Anita away, but when she came home he was filled with overwhelming ecstasy. As far as

George Andrew was concerned, he had Drucilla to play with when Buck was busy at the bank. When Anita came home, Drucilla resented it.

After an extended six-month tour in Hong Kong, Anita came back to Paris and promised Buckley that she would try to limit her excursions to France. Buckley went to her first return performance at the Paris Opéra. He had sat through the opera very still, and when Anita took her last bow, she put her hand to her brow; it was a gesture Buckley remembered very well—a signal she was weary of singing and ready to make love in her exhausted state, as if the thrusting act could revive her strength and vitality.

But perhaps, he thought, the gesture was not as meaningful as he had remembered. On the stage now, under the charged lighting, Anita looked suddenly drawn, anguished, and then, with a last lifting of the arm she made a mocking, ironic twist of the mouth. The curtain dropped and the houselights came on.

After Anita was dressed, she met Buckley at the Opéra Café. Buckley looked up from his glass as if viewing the past. She was unwashed, with her hair dirty; her clothes were the sort of stuff singers wear in second-rate nightclubs. She was very thin and had large bags under her eyes. Buckley asked if she was ill, and she just shrugged it off and nervously looked away. He knew not to ask any more questions or she might fly off in a rage. So they drank their coffee in silence and went home.

Chapter Twenty-six

The crew was lowering the jackhammers and the gas engine to power them in order to break through the frost. George put his head in his hands to clear his mind. The entire evidence of Silas Punt's idea of prehistory was there, waiting for him to dig it up.

On deck, Silas and the captain were watching the lowering of the gear into a launch. It was too dangerous to move the ship any closer to the ugly black outcroppings of sharp-toothed rocks. There was no inlet to serve as a harbor. Just an unwelcoming shoreline of gravel and black sand.

As he stood on the deck of the *Enterprise* about to go onshore at Sarichef, George wondered if he was any better off here than in the jungle in the Korean War. He had now been on four digs and was well known for his photography work.

When they landed at Sarichef, Silas decided to dig inland away from the beach. Silas continued his pacing while George remained patient. He had been on enough digs to know that they sometimes took days—even weeks. In one of the tents pitched near the beach, he sat with the captain while the jackhammers rumbled outside.

On the second day at the site, one of the men found an odd-shaped bit of black stone.

Silas was overjoyed. "See, see! Rough primitive flint! Keep digging!"

George examined the bit of stone. "I don't think it's anything. It's just a piece of boulder."

"No, George. I tell you, you are blind. There is man's engraving on this flint."

"If so, he must have been a clumsy bastard. No, Silas, I think your imagination's getting hold of you."

"Don't move from that spot. Dig!"

On the third day, they were three feet underground. A windstorm came in and knocked down the tents, and they all returned to the ship.

"A lousy sign," said George. "It's too early for a storm."

"A good omen," said Silas. "The people during such weather would have to stay here for a longer time."

George awoke to find the storm was over. They went ashore and pumped the water out of the pit.

In the afternoon George, standing knee-deep in mud, came across a smooth stone that was clearly the head of an ax. Silas was mad with joy. He danced up and down. "Keep digging! We've hit the bonanza!"

The sun began to set, and the dusk was closing in on the crew.

"The light's bad," George said.

"Keep digging!" cried Silas. He leapt into the pit and began digging with his hands.

"The men are tired, Silas."

"Look, I've been here before. It doesn't really get too dark."

George was aware that some kind of hysteria was possessing Silas. Soon they found fragments of small crude pots with scratchy decor. George was cold, wet and his feet were frozen, and he was about to give up for the day when he found it—a small female figure of stone, a crude sculpture of a very fat woman with huge breasts and very wide hips. Silas let out a cry and grabbed it from George's hands. His whole body trembled.

"A fertility figure! Look at it! Look at it! The first Eve. The eternal womb."

It looked like sandstone, and George had seen several like it in various museums. It was certainly a primitive fertility image with its huge breasts and vast, sagging buttocks.

Silas carefully took it back to the ship, washed it and put it on a small table while the crew just sat and stared at it. Finally, Silas Punt's expedition was worthwhile.

"Tomorrow," Silas said, "we will have to take new carbon tests on surrounding material." He hugged the little figure.

The next day they found a bone needle, some seashells shaped like fishing hooks and pieces of carbonized wood.

"Enough, enough! Let's go now. We'll leave markers, Silas."

The shock of success had changed Silas into a madman. He was making wild claims until George made him take a sedative and bundled him into his bunk. George had rigged up stronger lights in the main cabin to take more detailed photographs of the finds. There were hints of snow in the wet air, and he wanted to get away soon.

It was late by the time George had the lights set properly and the artifacts laid out on a huge piece of white cardboard. For some reason he felt queasy. Something was bothering him. What was it? There was no doubt these were original, genuine artifacts. But why was Silas so sure they were all of the same period? The fetish figure puzzled him for some reason. He picked it up and examined it from all angles. Clearly no fake. The whitish stone with yellow streaks had small black spots on its back that he hadn't noticed before. He looked closer, and with a pencil he began to draw thin lines connecting the spots. It was like a puzzle in a child's magazine he and Maude used to work out, going from dot to dot, and so on. At first nothing made sense. Erasing, he began again. He got what looked like an *A* and a *5* and part of a *7*. Jesus Christ! He sat back and took a sip of gin. He lit a pipe and smoked thoughtfully. His hands were shaking. He had come to a dreadful conclusion. The black dots were clearly remains of discovery markings made at the moment of a find. It was customary to list all finds for the records in this way. Someone had rubbed them off, destroying the markings on the figure. But some black dots had remained. So he had solved the puzzle of a crime. Silas had gotten hold of real artifacts and salted a spot on this damn island with them. Now he was rediscovering them and would present the world with his dazzling find. Silas, a scientific con man! George took another sip of gin and went to Silas's cabin. He woke the old man brutally, shaking him in his fury, knocking his head against the bunk frame until he yelled out.

"You dirty bastard. You fraud. You stinking, yellow-bellied fake!"

"What? What?" Silas groped for his glasses.

"Those artifacts. You stole them. Of course—you were on the Allied commission after World War II to recover objects from bombed-out museums and labs."

"Wait, George. Let me explain."

"You crazy old man! You motherfucking bastard! Don't you know you'd be found out eventually, anyway? All artifacts are photographed—someone would have exposed you. And what about me? My reputation would be ruined for life!"

"Please . . . don't hurt me . . ."

He slapped the old man and, for a moment, he thought of killing him. Silas Punt just lay on his bed whimpering like a sick dog. George gave him two powerful slaps across his face. He left the old man alone, gathered all the artifacts and tossed them into the sea, as far as he could throw them. Then he went back to his cabin and got drunk.

Chapter Twenty-seven

Despite a lower economy and continued turmoil in the oil industries, four of the nation's major banks yesterday reported higher second-quarter earnings. The one exception was Chemical National, whose earnings were down but had some encouraging aspects to them.

"As rates slid during the quarter, banks' cost of funds fell, but the interest that banks were earning on their loans did not fall as quickly," said Gregory Fiore of P-H. "The two underlying factors here are that fee momentum is strong even though there is no loan growth, and nonperforming loans are pretty stable."

Gregory read the report with pleasure. A little vanity does a man good, he thought, waving at the portrait of Old George facing him on the wall. It was good to see that he still was being treated as a major figure in national banking circles. When Gregory was a younger man, it was usually explained that Old George had left P-H in such fine shape that the bank ran on rails he had set up.

Although he hadn't voted for John F. Kennedy, Gregory and Stella had been invited several times to lunch at the White House.

Buckley called from Paris. "Europe has a wild hare up its ass over this Soviet missile crisis, Greg. You think the Russians will back down?"

"Damn if I know."

"How about our Pentland oil deal loan? If there's war, the Soviets will seize the whole damn Persian Gulf area."

Gregory looked at some notes on his desk. "How much have we figured to loan?"

"Two hundred and fifty million dollars. I think, Greg, we better keep it on ice till we see how the pendulum swings."

"If it swings wrong, Buck, we are all in the soup. I don't know how Kennedy thinks. Does he have balls? He's just sent a military 'council,' he calls it, to Vietnam. Damn the playboy."

"Greg, I think he'll hold firm, but let's wait and see. How's Stella and Bob?"

"Stella is fine. Bob has started right in at the bank, and he's doing beautifully. Anita and George Andrew okay?"

"Anita has left me, Greg. I'm very worried about her. I think she's been ill, but she just wouldn't talk to me about it."

"Look, Buck, maybe you're better off this way, you and George Andrew."

When the telephone call ended, Gregory sat studying the figures of the oil loans, thinking how simple it was in Old George's time. Anita had always been a mystery to Greg. From the start she was trouble for Buck. He wished he had thrown her desperate, lying letters away.

The next days were bad, and then as the president began to bunch his fleet around Cuba, the Russians began to pull out their missile bases. Somehow Gregory felt it was a time of fantasy, a series of games played with deadly toys.

He took Stella to dinner at the Top of the Mark, and they danced to "Moon River." Someone gave the bandleader five dollars to play a popular tune, "Love Makes the World Go 'Round."

"It's good to see you smiling," said Stella.

"Jesus, we have something to smile about. Nobody has set off the Doomsday Bomb. I feel old, honey."

The music ended, and at their table there was a bucket and a large bottle of very costly champagne. The wine steward smiled and twirled the napkin-wrapped bottle in its icy bucket.

Stella said he was drunk even before the bottle was uncorked.

In Paris Buckley was happy to be working out the oil loan, although Henri Satie, growing old and careful, warned against the Arabs continuing their raising of oil prices. "They can get a strangle hold on the European economy. *Mon Dieu!* If they decide to cut off supplies, what do you think will happen to Europe? We've been foolish enough to base most of our major economies on oil."

Gregory grinned. "What do you suggest? Going back to windmills?"

Henri was not taking chances the way he used to. He had become very conservative as he grew old. Pacific-Harvesters European business was all on Buckley's shoulders, with long-distance advice from Gregory. But Gregory was far away and not close to the action, so Buckley had buried himself in his work. His domestic life left something to be desired, and

George Andrew was not easy to get along with. In fact, Buckley thought he was spoiled. Miss Drucilla did try to keep a firm hand, but there were times, however, when he wondered if by nature he was cut out to be a father.

It was Saturday, and Miss Drucilla had taken George Andrew to the zoo. Buckley decided to take a long walk and stopped in a neighborhood café. He was finishing his coffee when a lean man in a wide hat and with a violin case under one arm came up to him, his face thin and creased, eyes large and bagged with a wrinkled skin darker than his cheeks.

"Signor Fiore?"

"Yes?"

The man seemed to look about, as if ready to bolt. Then his courage returned. With an accented English he said, "This is not my business, you undastan'? I am sometime the violin player in the Roma Opera."

"What is it?" Buckley was beginning to feel uncomfortable.

"This last month has been for opera not good. Your wife is in a room at the Hotel Casarina near the Porta Portese. She is very sick and refuses to go to the hospital." The man shifted his violin case to his other arm. "No one knows she is there or who she is." He bent lower, his voice almost a whisper. "But me. I was with her at La Scala. She doesn't know I've told you where she is."

Buckley felt something like an overwound clock spring tighten in his chest.

"Is this some kind of setup?"

"No, I am concerned about Anita. She has lost weight and looks very pale. She can no longer sing. I think she wants only to die. So she just wastes away. And now she stays in this dirty hotel by the Porta Portese."

Buckley tried to keep his mind clear of wonder and rage. Perhaps this was a kind of swindle. Buckley stood up and signed the chit. "Enough. Take me to the hotel."

The Casarina Hotel was just as dirty as the man had described it—its front-door plate glass was repaired with tape. They walked right into Anita's room. A low-powered light bulb partly covered with green paper gave some vague illumination to a wretched little room. One window shade was partly drawn. There was a black crucifix on the door, and the wallpaper showed the remains of bugs that had been crushed by many who had rented this room in the past. On a narrow bed Buckley made out a bundle of rags. Closer, as he stood under the crucifix, he saw that it was the outline of a woman under old clothes, a narrow gray blanket and a worn fur jacket.

Anita turned from facing the wall and looked up at him. Her face was feverish and damp, her eyes seemed unable to focus on Buckley. Her lips made a weak-muscled gesture as if preparing to speak. But no words came out.

He said, "Anita," and bent over the bed.

The voice was thick. "Buy us a drink, sport." Her words were feeble, grainy. "Overture in five minutes . . . damn the draft . . . singing tonight? . . . oh, *Der Rosenkavalier* . . . hire the car to Biarritz . . . champagne . . . oh, God . . . *la cosa marcha* . . . dying Egypt, dying . . ."

Her mouth remained open, and she was looking past him as if blind, not reacting to him being there in the room.

"It's Buckley, your husband."

"Who, what? . . . no interviews tonight . . . please. Had such a long season . . . tired, darling, tired, *ah, baron, es de vidrio la mi mujer* . . . so tired, bet your sweet ass I'm tired . . . two encores . . . such roses . . . so tired . . ."

A small tear fell from Buckley's face onto her pillowcase.

Chapter Twenty-eight

The hospital in Paris took Anita right away as an emergency patient. Buckley Fiore paced about in its second-story waiting room. He could recall the ambulance that had brought him and Anita to this place, the wild traffic parting to the siren like the Red Sea. Now in the waiting room, he just sat silently, looking at the sterile white walls. A brisk young doctor came through the swinging doors.

"Ah, Monsieur Fiore. I know this waiting is difficult for you. I am Dr. Ambrosi. Anita is very weak from not eating, and her pulse is slow."

"How ill is she, really?"

"Unfortunately her heart and lungs are weak. She will have to be in bed for a long time." Dr. Ambrosi shook his head. "Physical condition is all I can diagnose. She will need mental help. Maybe you ought to take her far away—maybe to a sanitorium where she can be properly cared for."

"She's led an eccentric life. I'd rather keep the diagnostic shrinks away."

"She is mentally ill, Mr. Fiore."

He put out his cigarette in a brass ashtray. "But as I say, I'm out of my field here. When her health is in better condition, I'll recommend some good doctors to you who specialize in psychoanalysis and neurology."

"Can I see her?"

"In half an hour. The nurses are bathing her right now. Clearly she hasn't bathed for some time."

"How soon can she travel?"

The doctor looked surprised. "You have not been listening to me. This is a very disturbed woman. Her body is weak, and we don't know what the blood tests will show."

Buckley pulled himself together, shook his head. The doctor left after a handshake, and Buckley sat down in a wicker chair, his knuckles pressed against his mouth.

The nurse came in. "Mr. Fiore, your phone call to Mexico has come in." She handed him the phone.

"*Merci*. Hello, hello. That you, Nat?"

"Buck! It's you, really you. I'm about to cast off for Aztos in two days. I'd be glad to take a look at Anita for you. Sounds pretty bad."

"Nat, that would mean the world to me. I think I need to get away from Paris with her. She'll remember your houseboat from the honeymoon—it left her with only good memories."

"Never mind that. Get a car and get to my boat pronto. It's in Nice—243 Quai Papacino, dock 55 under the bridge."

"Okay. What's the name of your boat?"

"The *Circe*. Look, I must hang up now. I look forward to seeing you and Anita."

He was relieved to hear Doc Rosegold's voice again. But how was he going to get Dr. Ambrosi to sign Anita's release?

Buckley felt a release of pressure, felt almost elated and yet very tired. There was still so much to do. He convinced Dr. Ambrosi to sign a certificate that Anita was in proper shape to leave the hospital, and he even agreed to accompany the private ambulance to Nice and to the yacht.

The last late-night report on Anita's condition was that she was resting under sedation. The next morning Anita was gently snoring in the hospital bed. There were some obscene red tubes leading into her arm. Her condition was improving, the nurse proudly reported. The blood pressure was better, and she had used the bed pan.

But she did not know Buckley when she opened her eyes. She just looked out as if from a hazy window at a world she showed no interest in. She was not showing any reactions. It was as if she preferred to live inside a cloud where she didn't have to talk to anyone. Her eyes looked huge and blank. Buckley looked down at Anita as two nurses prepared her for the journey to Nice. She silently permitted herself to be handled and dressed.

An attendant said the ambulance was ready, and Dr. Ambrosi waited outside. The trip to Nice was uneventful. Buckley had asked the driver not to use the siren, and he sat with the doctor facing Anita, who was strapped onto a low platform.

She was again lightly sedated but opened her eyes from time to time. Buckley thought Anita had a better color, and the doctor agreed but said that it was the result of the liquids they had been dripping into her arm.

"I have heard her sing, Monsieur Fiore. She probably will not be able to perform again. Her lungs are rotting and weak. I don't think she'll ever recover her voice completely."

"All I have left are a few recordings."

He didn't mind the doctor talking about Anita. Somehow it made the trip real, and brought back memories of the way she once had been.

They finally arrived at the yacht early in the morning. Nat Rosegold greeted them and helped Dr. Ambrosi get Anita settled in her cabin bed. When he got back on deck with Buckley, he said, "Poor Buck. Her condition looks very bad. Don't worry, we'll do everything we can to help her."

The *Circe* sailed steadily with her two powerful engines. Nat Rosegold knew ships and how they were built, and she was well handled. *Circe* was a bit on the fancy side, a costly pet. The crew were all from Greece, even the cook.

Anita lay in a fine cabin of teak and bronze, with two portholes above her bed. She was in that state between nearly waking and calm sleep. She made no sign she knew Buckley, and on the second day out he gave up talking to her, trying to coax her back to reality.

As they drew near the island, Buckley felt doubts and certain pressing fears. He had sent off cheerful letters to George Andrew, Gregory and Henri Satie—messages that said Anita had come back to him and they decided to take a cruise with Doc Rosegold for a kind of second honeymoon.

On the last day of the journey, he went below and sat by Anita's bedside. She had recovered much of her color, and her face had filled out. Anita had been able to be led by the steward to the bathroom. But she didn't speak, and once back in bed, she took up her rigid posture.

Buckley reached for one of her hands and pressed it, recalling a little game of tickle and pressure they used to play when feeling silly and amused at themselves. She kept her eyes closed, her lips began to quiver and she attempted sound. Her voice was low and far away. "B sharp, maestro," she said, "a half cadence . . ."

That was all she said before sinking back to her own little world.

Chapter Twenty-nine

It was two hours before the *Circe* could clearly be made out, a beautiful sight, its trim lines cleaving the sea. Its deck trim and spars made it a modern work of art. The yacht's rotating radar, Doc Rosegold felt, was a searching cosmic eye hunting the truth where there was no truth.

Savros, one of Nat Rosegold's servants, stood on the bridge as the yacht slowly made for the Aztos's only pier. Buckley came on deck leading Anita, followed by the doctor. Anita wore black slacks, a yellow sweater and black ballet slippers. A sailor followed with several bulky bits of baggage.

"Ahoy, there!" shouted Savros. Doc Rosegold waved back. A chauffeur opened the doors of the station wagon. Carefully Buckley led Anita ashore.

Savros remembered Anita and Buckley from the honeymoon and shook their hands.

"Welcome, welcome." Savros smiled at her, acting as if nothing had changed.

"Savros, help the sailor with stowing the luggage."

Soon they were all seated in the station wagon, and it took off, its gears growling up the rise in the road. Buckley gently held Anita's hand. She seemed to be completely unaware of the fine island scenery. The chauffeur offered Doc a cigar. The car went up the climb slowly and then quickly. The island was well cultivated, and here and there they passed some goats. Far to the left were hilly fields, with rows of olive and citrus fruits and walnuts. Far up in the hills were rows upon rows of grapevines.

Anita remained silent, and Buckley hoped she was at ease. How could it be that they were such strangers to each other? He supposed he never really knew Anita. It was a mistake to force her to fit into his lifestyle—to try to raise a family.

The car turned past a well-kept lawn, and below they saw a shelf of beach. They drove onto the houseboat, which stood next to a sea cliff. Savros got out and began to drag the bags out of the car. A man well over six feet tall with a rusty beard came out and stood on the deck of the houseboat.

"J. E. B. Stuart." His voice was measured, calm and even warm. "Welcome to our island."

Doc did the honors of introductions. "Prince, these are our guests. Mr. Fiore"—he winked at Buckley—"and Miss Anita."

"Charmed to have you with us," said the man.

Doc Rosegold added in French in an aside to Buckley, "The Prince is crackers but harmless. A very sweet man and a good friend."

Annie, Doc Rosegold's nurse, appeared, arms folded and wearing a yellow sweater over her white skirt. "The rooms be ready. If the lady will follow me."

Anita pulled her hand from Buckley's grasp and moved over to the large blond woman. Without looking back, she followed Annie into the house.

Doc said it was the hour of cocktails. The sun was slanting to the west. The dining hall was a vast room with its original rough-hewn rafters, and the walls had new plaster repairs among fragments of a mural.

Savros acted as butler, aided by two dark young women from the village on the other side of the island. Doc Rosegold, Buckley and the Prince sat down at the table for dinner. Buckley praised the chicken curry.

They drank a pale, rose-colored wine and talked mostly about Anita. Over the dessert, apple pie and wedges of yellow cheese, the Prince brought up a sex problem of a friend of his, "très outré." Doc said if his friend would come visit the island, he'd listen to her. "But I don't hand out advice to a relay team."

After dinner Buckley went up to Anita's room. He gave her a kiss on the cheek. Anita gave no reaction. He got up and closed the door behind him.

Buckley and Doc Rosegold retired to what Doc called his lab. It consisted of crude shelves, towers of old magazines on the floor and files that leaked folders. They sat in well-worn but comfortable club chairs around a large, green-shaded lamp.

"What do you think of Anita, Doc?"

"You've been through the ringer, haven't you?"

They lighted pipes and blew smoke. Doc leaned back, crossed his legs and looked up at the ceiling.

"I'm not a Park Avenue quack who gives a five-minute rub of your belly and sends in a bill for a thousand dollars. Most modern medicine is a fraud. It keeps you alive longer when you're long past ready to go."

"Goddamn it, Doc, cut it out. What about Anita?"

"Anita? I haven't had the chance to look at her closely. I'll examine her tomorrow."

Buckley rubbed his chin, felt his nose. "She's very sick."

Doc laughed and blew out a mouthful of smoke. "Don't teach me my trade, Buck. You're not the doctor. You could drag her over land and sea to the Freudian couches, feed her Jung and Adler. If she's gone, we'll have to get her back. It's more than nerves with her. I'll know better in a few days."

After a few hours of talking about Anita, Nat Rosegold stood up, yawned and looked at a wall clock. "Getting late, gotta get up early."

It left Buckley dissatisfied. Damn Doc. There had to be details, more reasoning of things out. Doc sounded more like Groucho's patter than a psychiatrist.

Chapter Thirty

Buckley stayed on at Aztos and decided against any communication with Gregory, Maude, George, Andrew or Henri Satie.

Anita ate, slept and took walks with Buckley or Annie or the Prince. Doc Rosegold continued his treatments in the lab, and Anita was showing gradual improvement. The only ones she talked to were Doc Rosegold and the Prince. She remained silent with Buckley. Doc Rosegold asked Buckley to avoid her as much as he could, especially during her treatments.

One afternoon Buckley could not resist going in to Anita's bedroom.

She sat on a chair, rubbing the damp ends of her hair with a towel, her head tilted to one side. She was surprised to see Buckley staring at her from the doorway.

"I believe you must know something of what is going on around you. I mean, even if Doc is helping you, why don't you want to talk to me, damn it! You owe me something!

Something! For bringing you here, for loving you and devoting nine years of my life to you.

She gave no reaction.

He screamed, "Anita!"

She dropped the towel and went back to a deeply catatonic blankness. Buckley wanted to apologize, but Annie came rushing in and scooted him out of the room, closing the door behind her.

Buckley felt desperate. He went to take a long walk on the beach and was met by the Prince. To avoid talking about Anita, he asked, "Are you a true prince?"

The Prince waved a finger at him. "Every man can be a prince if he's born in the right bed, in front of a witness, of course."

Buckley didn't push the question.

He helped the Prince award the stars and crosses of loyalty second-class to some fishermen repairing their nets on the beach.

Walking back to the houseboat, he suddenly said to Buckley, "May an older man advise you? You will never solve your problem here."

"What problem, Prince?"

"Anita. I observe. I know these things. In a way, she is like me. We are, she and I, suspended between sky and earth. And our illusions are our reality. Forgive me, my friend. I should not interfere in your world. Presumptuous of me . . . I have too much on my mind." They walked silently back to the houseboat and said nothing to each other at dinner.

One day Doc found Buckley sitting on the edge of a sea cliff. The tide was going out with splashing sounds on the rocks two hundred feet below, exposing the kelp-covered shore.

"The last jump is never worthwhile, Buck." Doc was standing beside him, hands in pockets.

"You're nuts. I wasn't going to jump."

Doc sat down beside Buck. "It's my theory eighty percent of all suicides, not those caught in a terminal illness, happen because of ego and vanity."

"Fuck you, Doc. I'm sick of your ironic indifference."

Buckley tried to get up, but the doctor pulled him down. "This is a final report on Anita, and as you're paying for it, hear me out. I put nothing in writing."

"Go away, Doc. Just send your bill."

"Anita is complex, and I'm only giving a surface reading. Deep in her subconscious she regressed to childhood losses. So, when she began to fail as a singer, she stomped down her failures and developed an inner division to suppress that failure. She couldn't face her failure as a singer, a wife and a mother. You follow me, Buck?"

"Sure, but where does that leave Anita? And what about me? This is one big mess for me."

"Don't brag. You're not that important as to have a clue to her condition. In fact you were a dagger stabbing at her when you reappeared."

"She would have died there in that run-down hotel."

"Not really. Hotels don't like people dying in their rooms."

"Is she getting better?"

"Not when you're around her. I don't know if she'll ever be herself again. She definitely won't sing—the voice is gone. Maybe she'll stay here with Annie and me. She's showing some interest in the Prince, and that's a start for her recovery. She enjoys it here, Buck. You're just a constant reminder to her of her failures."

"You mean I should leave her here?"

"Go home, Buckley. Get the hell off my island. There is an olive-oil buyer coming in two days by copter to bid on the crop. He can give you a ride. I'll keep in touch regarding her progress. If and when she's ready to deal with her past, I'll let you know."

Buckley left the island of Aztos two days later in the olive-oil buyer's copter. Anita was in the grove, and he didn't see any sense in a last goodbye.

Buckley heard from Doc Rosegold a month after he left Aztos:

My dear Buck,

Thank you for the check. As to Anita—she is making progress, and by that I don't mean she will ever be what she was in her prime. She remains not much of a talker but we can understand what she says. She is picking olives and making new friends in the village. She laughs and sings up there among the olive trees, and they sit around little fires and cook up peppery garlic messes and drink wine. She must recall her childhood in Mexico when she is with these people.

The Prince sends his regards to you. Savros has just sent you a fresh batch of cigars. I hope, Buckley, that you are back in the proper groove in your life pattern.

Keep in touch,
Nat

Chapter Thirty-one

"I've decided what I want to do, Dad."

"You'll come help us at the bank?"

"If you still want me."

"Damn it, George. We've always wanted you here at the bank. But then you turned your back on us for some dream you were reaching for."

"Well, Dad, what I wanted just didn't pan out, I guess. The bank can have me—lock, stock and barrel."

George and Gregory were seated on the little balcony overlooking the Pacific swells crashing into the rocks on which Cliff House stood. Gregory felt the deep, penetrating comfort of the summer sun on his body, like a cozy hug. At last, George was back with him.

A young man in a white houseman's jacket came out carrying a tray with frosted Tom Collinses on it.

"Ah, Jimmy . . . thanks," said Gregory with a yawn. "George, this is Jimmy Hutton—Cody's nephew."

"How's old Cody doing up in Oregon?" asked George as he

took a long sip from his drink.

"Just fine. He's raising horses and fishing for salmon. Doing whatever he feels like doing, I guess."

After Jimmy left, Gregory and George sat for a while longer, quietly looking out over the water. Gregory pursed his lips and nodded as if the past were coming back. "I remember when I traveled down to Texas with your grandfather Charles. P-H had put up a lot of money for an oil dig in a town called New Brandy. My dad and Old George had been at odds for a long time. My father was in charge of the bank's interest in that well. Jesus, George, I was there when she blew in—the great Sky Dome well. The site became the greatest oil strike of its time. My father's health was not good and he died soon after. So I closed the chink in the generation gap and moved from a boomtown to a banker's office. Your great uncle Fred, Buckley's pop, ran our movie-studio loans. What about you, George? Have you thought about what path you want to take—a niche, so to speak?"

"Well, Dad, I'm a bit fed up with outdoor adventure. In digging up the past you have to have luck as well as skill. I won't find a King Tut's tomb—or the earliest skull ever turned up in Africa. I just don't seem to have that kind of luck or perseverance. Every expedition I got hooked into turned out to be a failure."

"Take it easy for a while, George. Go find a girl and get married."

Inside a clock bonged. It was late afternoon and Gregory and George watched the sun go down from Cliff House as the ocean continued to assault the cliff.

George spent the next week visiting friends and taking out the old sailboat that Buckley used to roam the bay with. All he wanted was peace and quiet and to clear his mind of Silas

Punt and the damn stolen artifacts. He had to push away all the expectations that had held promise and didn't seem to get him anywhere.

Gregory had been aware that his son's mood was at a point where his nature was pliable. If he could just mold George into the family pattern so he could perform the necessary duties that would be demanded of him at Pacific-Harvesters, George would have a goal—something to get him back on track after those last years of hardship and disappointment.

Stella introduced George to some girls from the Bay area— the eligible single daughters of important families in the community. Gregory was constantly on the phone to Paris ironing out George's future with Henri and Paul Achille.

One day, over breakfast, Gregory said, "I've got something in the hopper that might work out for you—with your approval, of course. Henri Satie is going to retire from the Paris office in six months. I'd like you to go over there and let him show you the ropes. Of course, Buckley will continue to run P-H in Paris for a few more years. But by the time Buckley is ready to come back here and run the show for me once I'm ready to retire, he can train Bob to be his right-hand man. I'm hoping that by the time Henri Satie is ready to retire, you and Paul Achille can run the show in Paris."

"But Dad—you, Buckley and Henri Satie are pretty tough acts to follow."

"You will do a fine job, son. In your own way, you are just as capable of running P-H as any of us—maybe a different management style, but just as effective."

After breakfast, Gregory and George went sailing and talked some more about George's future with the bank.

"So, George, how do you feel about everything we've talked about?"

"Paris? Learning the ropes? I feel good about it but a little scared. But that's only natural, I guess. And I feel like I'll be competing with Bob, and he's already trained through the ranks in the bank—he's ambitious and I'm not so sure I can do as good a job as he can."

"Bob may be ambitious, George. But you are the creative one in the family. Don't think of competing with Bob. Just think of what a well-polished machine you and he will make of old P-H. You'll both be contributing your own special talents to the organization—breathe new life into it. Hey, I'm meeting Stella in the afternoon for some cocktail affair. Want to come along? I hear there will be some gorgeous young debutantes who are really excited about meeting you. You're the toast of the town."

George watched the club dock and judged the slow movement of the sailboat toward the marina. "I think I'll skip this one, Dad. I've got to do a lot of thinking *all by myself.*"

A yacht-club boat attendant came forward to catch the mooring line. On the shaded porch members waved at Gregory. George thought, What will the archaeologists in a thousand years find here? A hundred feet of concrete dock, a dozen cocktail glasses and the shell from a lobster thermidor . . .

Chapter Thirty-two

Gregory and Stella watched the news on television report the bombing of North Vietnam after claims that an American destroyer had been attacked in the Gulf of Tonkin. Gregory called Buckley, who reported to Gregory that he had talked to the French ambassador, home from a vacation in Tokyo, who said that no one could verify the attack—not even the Pentagon.

"Greg, the French are saying the attack story was conjured up to panic Congress for a resolution to send our troops into the war."

"Come on, Buck. Lyndon Johnson is one smart cookie. He would not put his ass into a bear trap like that."

"The parties in Washington are whooping it up. Look what it's doing to the morning's market."

"Christ. I hate to think we're dumb enough to walk into this one."

"Meanwhile, we've got to sort out our overseas loans. You know how bad news breeds unrest. How's Stella and Bob?"

"Bob's working at the bank and doing a fine job. He's got a girlfriend, and they're living together. Can you believe this new generation? How's George doing at the Paris branch? You and Henri Satie training him properly?"

"His work is okay—he'll just take a little while to catch on. It's amazing how he's taken to living in Paris. He's a great social success. He brings in clients and good business—he really knows how to entertain the customers. What a diplomat!"

Gregory just said he hoped George wasn't goofing off too much.

Gregory was wrong, he admitted, about North Vietnam. As the war spread in Vietnam, it became apparent that this was to be a major American war. Pacific Harvesters had to tighten its banking methods and rethink its loans. Gregory had let others run their departments independently, and now he began to wonder if he had placed more trust in his people than he should have. Gregory remembered a conversation he had recently with Chester Wetlock, one of the chief brokers.

"We handle this in our own way," Gregory snapped.

"But it's over four million dollars!"

"We'll absorb it. You understand write-offs, Chester. You know the banking system and you know P-H would never do anything illegal. A mistake was made by one of our officers, and believe me, he will be out on his ass tomorrow. So we write off the loss." Gregory smiled calmly.

"Fine. But Mr. Fiore, if I may say so, there is such a thing as having too much loyalty to employees," Chester sniffed.

Gregory had always trusted Chester Wetlock's reports—but sometimes, he thought, he just didn't have a good sense of diplomacy. Chester just felt Gregory was well past his prime.

Gregory asked Buckley and George to come back to San Francisco for two weeks to help work out some figures, after which the bank issued a statement to the business media.

PACIFIC-HARVERSTERS CREATES UNIT
FOR FOREIGN LOANS PROBLEM

The special-loan subsidiary will attempt to deal with the bank's nearly half billion dollars in nonperforming and restructured loans in Third World countries. P-H has suffered substantial losses by creating a team of experts under the bank's chief officer for Latin America, Buckley Fiore. The bank announced that it had formed a similar unit to handle troubled domestic business and consumer loans.

The meeting in Gregory's office was attended by Buckley and George and the two lawyers who had replaced Joe Dalgaard, who had recently retired from P-H. Robin Kune and Leo Weingarten were specialists in corporate law.

Weingarten approved of P-H cutting back on loans because of the bad years of South American banking. "The nation has been down there backing the fat cats against the people. But it's not going to stay that way. Complete withdrawal is our only answer."

George tapped his cigarette ash off in an ashtray. "Easy for you to say, Leo. Know how they catch monkeys in Siam? They put a banana in a jug with a narrow mouth—just enough to get the monkey's hand in. He goes for the banana, grabs it and can't get his hand out without dropping the fruit. He doesn't drop the banana, Leo, so he's caught. You see, we've got our hands in the jug in several different places and we can't let go. If we and a few other big banks take our hands out and try to call in all loans, there will be worldwide panic."

Robin Kune rubbed his lower lip. "Best not to cover up too much. Give out your version of the bank's situation as calmly as possible. Then wait."

Buckley said, "So, gentlemen, we'll just wait."

When the Fiores were alone together, Gregory tapped on his desktop with a letter opener until Buckley took it away from him.

"Settle down, Greg. The bank has been through the rapids before this."

"Yes, but not with me in command. Frankly, I don't feel I'm handling this properly. Somehow I don't feel I can go on without stripping my gears. It's time for me to step aside and let you make the big decisions."

"Horseshit," snapped Buckley. "Let things stay as they are, and we just put up a very calm front. We close seventy-five of the banks that aren't shining their brightest. We skim the fat off the staffs—most of them don't work anyway."

George was staring at the ornate Persian rug, trying to follow its pattern. "We've got to draft a statement on our expected losses. Show we have nothing up our sleeves. To the *Times* and *Wall Street Journal*—all the press, in fact."

The following morning the report was released to the press:

PACIFIC HARVESTERS REPORTS LOSSES

The nation's third largest bank has raised its estimate for loan losses by $100 million, according to those who have talked recently with bank officials. Provision for losses has been raised to $1.2 billion from estimates of two months ago.

"We have slightly increased our outlook for loan losses for the year," says Buckley Fiore, chief financial officer. He declined to give any figures. Losses throughout the bank's loan portfolio totaled $1 billion last year, producing a record loss for the company.

Gregory felt he was really beginning to slip away from the harsh realities taking place at the bank. Although he was aware of his losses, he always had faith in the men who had run up those huge losses. Clearly he had lost a lot of the control that his grandfather George had built up for him at P-H, and for the first time he felt really worried about the future of the bank and of his family.

Back in his office the next morning, his secretary handed him his mail. A memo from Rumple, Cartell, and Wetlock—the accountants. He read it slowly.

To: Gregory Fiore, Esq.
Re: Unauthorized withdrawal of over $2 million

Our investigation has disclosed that a top officer may have made unauthorized withdrawals of millions from customer accounts in South America. Sources disclose he is Naldo Ruiz, forty years old, senior vice president for South American operations. Mr. Ruiz would not comment as to when he had made any withdrawal from customers' accounts, authorized or unauthorized.

Meanwhile, we can show that the money was not diverted for legitimate corporate purposes but rather for personal use.

We recommend these findings be transmitted to the United States Attorney's office and that the head of the criminal division make a preliminary inquiry.

Please advise.

Gregory put down the report and called Chester Wetlock, who told him the matter would have to go to Supreme Court.

"No, no Chester, we can't go to court with this—we've got to keep a low profile right now."

"Look, Gregory, we've got to face this. Our reputation is involved."

After a long discussion with Chester, Gregory hung up the phone feeling confused and tired.

He picked up *The Wall Street Journal* and on the front page was that damn press release again:

"Consumer losses continue to grow, as do agriculture and real estate," Gregory Fiore told the press. "In the future corporate relationships increasingly will be built on a financial institution's ability to provide both information and transaction services with credit, capital markets and other services arising from these relationships."

George Fiore has been named head of new corporate payments of the bank's world banking division under Buckley Fiore and Henri Satie, Chief Operations Officer. He will continue to help large corporate customers handle European transactions worldwide.

Stella decided to cheer up the family bankers by cooking a beautiful dinner. After they ate—mostly in silence—they were all so exhausted that they went right to bed before Jimmy Hutton could even clear the table.

Gregory and Stella now had separate bedrooms. They missed the warm intimacy of sharing a bed, but Gregory suffered from insomnia and spent the silent hours of the night reading. He would doze off around three in the morning and then around five he would try to get an hour of sleep before the alarm clock rang and he had to get dressed and ready for work.

Gregory wished he could think quickly and make decisions under pressure like he used to. He just didn't want to lose his dignity now—in the midst of one of the bank's biggest crises. He felt lucky to have Stella and his sons and daughters caring for him. They were what made his life bearable right now. But there were cracks in the changing world, and the cracks were quickly widening.

The bank was in real danger, as was his family's position.

The burdens were getting too heavy. The silent night and the dark house offered no answers to Gregory. There was a rustle of movement in the hallway, and Stella came in, her hair loose and hanging over her shoulders. She was wearing her rose-colored dressing gown, which had always been Gregory's favorite.

"Are you all right, Gregory?"

"I'm fine, darling. Go back to bed."

"Did you take your pills?"

"I only took half a pill. When I take a whole one it makes me too groggy to face the day ahead."

She leaned over and hugged her husband, kissing the top of his head. Her warmth and yielding body had always been so satisfying for him. She made him feel so comfortable and at peace with himself.

She reached over and turned off the desk lamp. "Try to sleep just a little while more, dear."

Gregory just nodded as she got into the bed with him. He wanted to express to her how much love he felt for her. But, he thought, it was something that was understood and didn't need to be said.

Chapter Thirty-three

It was a week later, and on the stock exchange there was a notable increase in the buying of Pacific-Harvesters shares. It was a puzzle, since Gregory and the P-H board had begun closing those banks that were not doing their share of the business or were located in declining neighborhoods where land values were worth more than the structures built on them.

Buckley rushed over from Paris for another meeting with the lawyers.

Gregory was worried and showed it. "I have a feeling that someone is piling up our shares. But why?"

Leo Weingarten adjusted his gold-rimmed glasses and took out some notes from his dispatch case. "Our New York office has obtained some information. Several companies are suspected of being fronts for one large company which is buying up a huge portion of P-H stock."

"Well? What large company, Leo?"

"McCall-Lazar International. They're private bankers—

corporate raiders. Ken McCall is the brain behind everything they do."

"Are they really so big? What are their assets?" asked Buckley, who had been quietly riffling through Gregory's files.

"They get their backing from Arab oil and Swiss private bankers."

Gregory was deep in thought as he lighted a fresh pipe. "Do you think it's a takeover push?"

Buckley shrugged. "Wouldn't they have to control at least twenty percent of our shares? That's a lot. Can they swing it?"

"Hell, no," said Gregory, who had just been jotting down figures on his pad. "The Fiore family trust has ten percent, the Fiore Foundation has fifteen percent. And who knows how much is in investors' hands? I don't think they can do it."

Leo Weingarten adjusted his glasses again. "They may be trying for a buyout of their holdings. They might even offer it to you, force it on you to keep them from making trouble. Then they'll walk away with control of P-H's money."

"Damn them—I won't let this happen to me or the bank!" shouted Gregory.

"It's called the greenhouse game. They may not want control of P-H at all. It's one of Ken McCall's old ploys. He's done it with Nu-World Plastics and Continental Bray Electric."

"We can still beat them," Buckley said.

Gregory wondered. "We're in no position to buy them out. Where would we get the money?"

"Wall Street," said Leo Weingarten.

"Suppose they turn us down? Or want control in return for their subsidy?"

"Turn down Pacific-Harvesters? They'd have to be crazy!" Buckley snapped.

Leo Weingarten put his arm around Buckley's shoulder,

and said calmly, "Ken McCall is a powerhouse on Wall Street. You could put the family trust and Foundation shares up as assets."

"And," Buckley replied, "McCall-Lazar would grab them—or their stooges could if their assets are as high as they're rumored to be."

Gregory got up from his desk and began pacing the floor.

Leo Weingarten closed his dispatch case. "Let's just wait and see what develops. I don't think they have control of anything near enough to make a move at this time."

The meeting ended. After the lawyers left, Gregory and Buckley sat unhappily, drinking bourbon.

"Jesus, Buck, I feel as if I've stopped thinking. I can't believe P-H is in this bind. We're still solid. Old George ran into a situation like this once, and he beat them."

"That was a long time ago, Greg. The bank is so big now—too spread out. Then there is the South American trouble with real estate loans we have to write off."

"I just don't know the answer, Buckley. I'm too old to learn new dance steps. I just sense a hovering cloud about to drop over me."

Buckley sipped from his drink and tried to smile and appear as calm as possible in front of his old cousin.

"Listen, Greg. Kune and Weingarten are the best in the business, and Pacific-Harvesters means something in the banking world on the national scene."

"That's why, Buck, we're such fat game. Maybe I've been too sure of myself and the abilities of others. Banking has changed over the years. Maybe we haven't kept up with the new front-runners and their hard-hitting ways."

"No sense in blaming yourself for change, Gregory." But Buckley, too, had felt the bank had been too placid, like an empire that can't be challenged. He had tried to press his own ideas on Gregory and Henri Satie. But they were his seniors, and to disagree with their methods was disrespectful and pre-sumptuous. Yet he had toughened himself and studied the international finance scene, observed that great change was coming. The power of oil money floating over Europe and coming into America was a big factor. Japanese and German prosperity were factors, too. No one had expected that they would recover so well from their lost wars. But, looking at Gregory, Buckley decided it didn't seem the time to press these points on him.

Yes, Buckley saw his cousin was getting old and had lost that tough sureness he once had.

Gregory studied his cousin's face and decided against another drink. He emptied his pipe and hung it in a rack that held a dozen Dunhills.

"Leo Weingarten is a very clever man, and trustworthy for a lawyer. We'll just have to move very slowly and wait to see what the next move will be from Ken McCall. Let's go have lunch, Gregory. I think I have to get away for a while—and I don't want to be alone."

They lunched at the Top of the Mark and talked about everything but the crisis at the bank. They talked about the beauty of San Francisco spread out before them—the dimpling bay and the bridges with strings tying them to the rest of the Republic.

It was after seven when Gregory got back to the bank. After parting from Buckley he had gone to the Bay Club to sit in its steamroom and have a massage. He fell asleep on the table.

Chapter Thirty-four

The week before there was to be a stockholders' meeting of Pacific-Harvesters shareholders, *The Wall Street Journal* ran another front-page story.

PACIFIC-HARVESTERS TAKEOVER IS RUMORED
BY MCCALL-LAZAR GROUP

While remaining among the top of the nation's banks, Pacific-Harvesters is showing losses in its far-flung national and international banking dynasty. Talk continues that raiders are nipping at its flanks for a takeover. Among those most prominent with assets to carry on the assault is Kenneth McCall, supported by McCall-Lazar International Corporations, with its great resources among Swiss private banks and Middle East oil money.

Pacific-Harvesters, with its huge assets and long history, has lately been struck by great losses from write-offs, real estate recessions, and Latin American loans. Four overtures by bargain hunters bidding for the Fiore fortress are looming.

Talk is that Ken McCall is in the best position to make a serious and successful bid for Pacific-Harvesters.

To fend off McCall-Lazar the West Coast branch will have to bring in a "white knight," someone with whom to form a merger strong enough to keep McCall from breaching and seizing the Fiore fortress. No knight appears in sight.

A secret meeting was called for in the dining room at Cliff House. The big dining-room table was extended to almost the length of the room.

Buckley, seated in the library, asked, "How many of the big holders are coming?"

"A lot of them," said Gregory. "Knewton is in Europe and the Canino twins are sailing somewhere in their yacht. However, we'll have enough for it to be a legal meeting."

"Paul Achille is coming with Satie family proxies. Maude, of course, and George."

Gregory looked at his watch. "Three o'clock," he said, adjusting his tie and wriggling his shoulders in his banker's gray. "Stella thought this suit looks like formal battle attire . . ."

"Oh, hell, Gregory, we're in fairly good shape."

"Fair shape, Buck? We've been buying P-H stock in self-defense, and even with the rumor of the state we're in, the price is holding steady."

"That's why Leo thinks it may be just a McCall buyout. He can make seventy-five million dollars easy as pie if he asks us to take up his holdings in P-H to get him off our backs. And after he cashes in, that's when we'll see a serious drop in stock."

Gregory swallowed two pills with a glass of water and grinned at the worried expression on Buckley's face. "It's a butterfly stomach—just keep your chin high and tail bushy."

Jimmy Hutton phoned from the hall that Mr. Weingarten was downstairs with Mr. Kune.

"Show them to the library, Jimmy," Gregory said with as much energy as he could muster.

Stella came into the library and, without saying a word, pressed a small blue flower into Gregory's lapel while Jimmy came in with Leo Weingarten and Robin Kune. He carried in a silver tea-and-coffee service, set it down on the small mahogony end table and poured everyone a cup of coffee.

Gregory looked at his watch again. "We have one hour before the board gets here, so let's discuss our strategy."

Leo, Robin, Buckley and Gregory all sipped their coffee, and Leo laid out several rows of papers. He used a pencil to point to important items, motioning like a conductor leading an orchestra.

"So I've had our scouts out digging around—put our people at the proper keyholes and our European contact is checking on what real credits are behind McCall-Lazar. Ken McCall has clout and he's loaded."

Buckley peered at the papers through his bifocals.

"Our plan," said Robin Kune, "is to concentrate on what we *think* McCall wants from us."

"Isn't it crystal clear? He wants Pacific-Harvesters," Gregory said with a sneer.

"Maybe. He has a big bite. But then again maybe he's not interested in a complete forceful takeover. Maybe he wants something else," Kune said in a very low voice.

Kune snapped shut a dispatch case and rubbed his fists together. He saw Gregory staring at him and then at Leo.

Leo said calmly, "Maybe he wants a place on the board. Maybe two places. A big say on our board about our methods and procedures to benefit his holdings. All very normal and legal."

"McCall on the board?" Buckley shouted. He was out-raged.

"Which plan do you think he'll move with?" asked Greg-ory.

"We just told you—all indications point to it," Kune said.

"If we have to," said Gregory, "then that's the plan we'll have to live with—the one that will cause the least amount of pain and harm to the bank. Two seats on the board, and we can hope to whittle them down to one."

"You two can handle his lawyers?" Gregory looked first at Leo and then at Robin.

"Handle? We can hold them at bay like a cage of tigers. I'll throw our last reserve of lawyers into it, and they'll bring up their line of Yale and Harvard prizefighters." Leo grinned.

From outside on the gravel driveway to Cliff House they could hear the first crunch of a car bringing four board mem-bers to the meeting.

Paul Achille and Maude arrived a half hour later. Maude insisted on bringing the twins to see "Grandpa Greg." Soon after they arrived, George came with two other board mem-bers. Then came Bob, and Penny had promised to show up after the meeting with her husband, Harry, who had just come back to Washington from a two-month piano tour.

"God! It's wonderful," Maude said, cheerfully greeting her father at the door with a big kiss and a hug. "Stella promised to help me keep the twins out of your way until the meeting is over." Stella came downstairs, and the twins jumped in her arms as she whisked them up to the big playroom to find kites to fly on the beach.

Finally all the board members had arrived and were seated

at the long dining-room table. Gregory's secretary was there
to take notes of every word spoken. But Buckley insisted
there be no tape recorders—just in case anything was said
that couldn't be erased easily.

For the first time, Gregory noticed how old the board members were. How foolish, even senile, some of them looked
next to George, Bob and Buckley.

"Let's proceed, gentlemen," Gregory began.

They discussed the possibility of McCall's takeover, its
consequences to the bank, and who owned what stock. Then
Leo Weingarten got his turn at bat. "This board is being
briefed so you will know the actual facts of our situation and
not what the media sees fit to distort. You have to accept that
P-H is in real danger and might be taken over by McCall-
Lazar interests. Our report of losses will be greater than ever,
and we will have to do what Wall Street calls "the turtle"—
pull in our collective necks. Gentlemen, you may be tempted
to sell your stock. Some of you have already sold some of your
holdings—never mind how we know. We have been buying
enough to keep a majority with what we have . . . and so let
me fill you in on how these takeover games are played . . ."

It was, Gregory felt, a good half hour before the properly
presented facts of their situation actually unfolded. Not one
of the board members fell asleep, and three members even
took notes.

The board meeting ended late in the afternoon with a good
solid buffet, cocktails and cigars. Maude and Stella went into
the city to meet Penny and Harry.

Leo Weingarten and Buckley went down to the garden to
smoke their cigars.

"Level with me, Leo. Give me your best guess at what
Ken McCall wants."

"Jesus, Buckley. I know the bottom line from one of my

head scouts. Two places on the board, and Gregory has to step down and become an inactive chairman of the board with little input in any real decisions."

"That son of a bitch!" Buckley said under his breath.

"Family loyalty is fine, and I love Gregory—an honorable man. But I think you know he isn't up to it anymore."

"Who becomes president then? One of McCall's men?"

"McCall wants you, Buckley."

Buckley looked at Leo as if he'd just been assaulted. When he spoke, it was with an ironic tone of controlled temper. "The bastard has his nerve."

The lawyer held up a hand and gave a hurt smile. "You think he's insulting you? Or seeing you as a sellout to the noble Fiore cause? Use your brain, Buck."

"Jesus, Leo. I don't understand you sometimes. You're our lawyer, not McCall's. And suddenly you toss this at me so matter-of-factly."

"Come on. Let's walk around the garden. You'll think more clearly while you're walking."

Buckley shrugged off Leo's offer and wondered how Gregory would feel when he heard the news.

"Look, Buckley, McCall isn't rubbing Gregory's nose in the dogshit by asking you to head P-H. He wants it to thrive with new ideas—and younger, bright people like you. He sees that it's getting old and rusty, but he doesn't want to take away the Fiore family stronghold."

Buckley sat down on the edge of an old stone fountain that had long since been dried up. No water had flowed from it for years. Birds had nested there once, raised their young and were now long gone. The few remaining nests consisted of disintegrating grass, twigs and crumbling leaves. Buckley remembered his days as a child racing around that fountain and swimming in it while Old George, his father, Charles and

Ramon would watch him and laugh, yelling, "Show-off!" He wished that fountain could flow again.

Leo broke the silence. "His game, Buck, is to use the Fiore name to keep the bank's reputation and shoot for a speedy recovery. Just remember that McCall does not and never will have the power of the Fiore name—and unlike Gregory, he has no family and no children."

Buckley studied the lawyer's face. "Just how the hell am I going to tell Gregory?"

"I think he probably already knows, Buckley. Flesh outlasts all, and generation after generation carries on. You have a son. Maude and Paul have children. George and Bob will get married someday and have children of their own, and Gregory understands the power of sons and daughters more than any of us. They will be there when the McCall-Lazar forces falter and go down in the dust. McCall-Lazar is not immortal, but the Fiore name will be."

Buckley began to laugh and he put his arm around Leo's shoulder.

"Greg wants out," Leo said seriously. "He isn't what he once was. You walk away from McCall's offer and someone else will step in, and then you will see a forceful takeover." He pulled out a large gold watch from his waistcoat and peered at it. "Gotta go. I have a date tonight. As Old George used to say, 'The cards are laid out on the table for play. Trust your friends, but before a deal cut the cards yourself.'"

They shook hands, and the lawyer walked up the garden path toward the steps to the terrace. A small breeze from the Pacific came across the garden, stirring neglected plants, removing a leaf here and there from old trees. Buckley just stared at the fountain. There was a crack in the stone, and the ants carried seeds and bits of debris, disappearing down the crack to some storage space for their goods.

Without thinking, Buckley lifted his foot and scraped it across the moving line of insects. He observed the dead ones and watched the line reform, the survivors taking their place in the procession. Several times he repeated his attack, slaughtering the booty-laden ants. He made no great impression, created no panic on the moving line of ants. Ignoring their losses, they marched on..

When Buckley stood up again, he felt refreshed and confident.

A breeze was turning into a strong wind. He recalled a rare Sunday sermon with Anita at the Paris embassy. "Go to the ant, thou sluggard," was its theme. Anita had invited the preacher to dinner, and the man got fuddled on brandy.

Buckley walked up to the house to talk to Gregory.

Epilogue

Gregory and Stella gave a big party in celebration of Buckley's promotion, as well as Gregory's seventy-first birthday. The orchestra played Gershwin tunes, and about a hundred guests showed up to drink to the happy event. The living room was set up like a ballroom with its great staircase, and the halls and surrounding rooms were blazing in amber light from crystal chandeliers of Tiffany stained glass. A dozen lampposts lighted the garden and driveway. The garden was illuminated like a movie set.

Stella had meant to keep the party to a reasonable number, but somehow it turned out to be much bigger than she'd expected. All the children were playing and screeching in the garden. Miss Drucilla had given up trying to control them.

Bob Fiore had announcced his engagement to a young woman, Ada, whom Gregory and Stella had just met for the first time—but they both agreed she was a fine young lady for Bob. As more guests arrived, Jimmy Hutton saw to it that the servants kept everyone well fed. Maude acted as hostess while Stella was upstairs helping Gregory dress for the event. Stella looked majestic in her bronze gown. She wore a tiara of gold filigree and pears on her reddish, graying hair, which was piled up on the top of her head with not one hair out of place. When Gregory was finally dressed and ready, Stella led him out of the bedroom and closed the door behind him.

Gregory stood in front of the French pier glass with Stella behind him, adjusting his tie. His fingers were stiff from arthritis. He looked at himself in the beveled glass mirror in the hall. There was a pattern to the lines on his face. His mustache was neatly trimmed by Jimmy Hutton. He was very old—just a shell of a handsome man. But he still had his teeth and a full head of silver hair.

"Okay, now, let's go, old man." Stella fixed the back of his jacket as they headed for the staircase.

"Did we have to have such a mob?" He touched his jade cufflinks and inhaled.

"Absolutely! Now, march." Stella smiled and kissed the back of his neck. "You're still a 'hunk,' as Penny always says."

He turned and kissed his wife's cheek and put his arm around her shoulder for support, and she could feel him tremble.

"Don't worry, Gregory. It's mostly family," she lied.

She had aged nicely, Gregory thought. Her eyes were clear and steady. Her body was still firm.

"My wild girl," he said tenderly.

"Come on. Stop stalling." She took his arm and moved him down the stairs. He didn't resist, just stiffened his aching spine and tried to step down with as much vigor as he could muster.

As he descended the stairs, he thought to himself, I suppose I am, in my own way, a religious man, even if I am a skeptic—to be able to believe in God and hope all my life. I've struggled with contradictions and inconsistencies. I suppose the solution is love for my family.

Everyone yelled at the bottom of the stairs, "Happy birthday!" Trays of champagne were brought in to toast Gregory, and everyone continued to celebrate, dancing and singing.

Yes, life would go on as long as the family continued to grow. Gregory continued his train of thought and barely realized that Penny and Maude were leading him across the room on each arm to talk to the other guests. Finally, he thought, I can rest in peace, knowing that my family really is immortal. That was Old George's dream, and it had come true. This was truly the happiest day of his life. He looked down into the garden from the huge living-room window and smiled at the fountain, which was once again flowing. The children were splashing and dipping their feet into the clear water.

Stella said to Jimmy Hutton, "Be sure you've opened enough champagne."